'The fire isn't out, Chris,' he stated, emphasising each word with painful clarity. 'You know that, only you won't admit it—yet.'

She pushed at his shoulders with determination.

'Adrian, please . . .' she muttered, dragging her mouth away. 'Do you want the patients to see?'

His lips were moist and his eyes heavily laden with desire. 'Chris, don't fight me,' he pleaded. 'Remember how it used to be? We can be like that again—happy . . . You're only hurting yourself this way.'

'No, *you're* hurting me!' she flashed. 'Let me go, Adrian!'

He ignored her pleas. He held her head against his chest, one large hand spread across her fiery cheek and she could feel his heart pounding faster than normal. After a moment he tilted her chin up and looked into her troubled grey eyes, 'I think you still love me, Chris,' he murmured.

She gave a small painful sob. If she told him she loved him, she would have to tell him the other truth as well . . .

Judith Worthy lives in an outer suburb of Melbourne, Australia, with her husband. When not writing she can usually be found bird-watching or gardening. She also likes to listen to music and the radio, paints a little, likes to travel and is concerned about conservation and animal cruelty. As well as romantic fiction, she also writes books for children. DOCTOR IN PRACTICE is Judith Worthy's thirteenth Doctor Nurse Romance.

# DOCTOR IN PRACTICE

BY

## JUDITH WORTHY

**MILLS & BOON LIMITED**
ETON HOUSE   18-24 PARADISE ROAD
RICHMOND   SURREY   TW9 1SR

First published in Great Britain 1988
by Mills & Boon Limited

© Judith Worthy 1988

Australian copyright 1988
Philippine copyright 1988
This edition 1988

ISBN 0 263 76259 9

Set in Times 10 on 10 pt.
03 – 8811 – 57244

Typeset in Great Britain by JCL Graphics, Bristol

Made and printed in Great Britain

# CHAPTER ONE

IT WAS a few minutes after nine a.m. when Dr Christine Hart drove into the car-park at Tullamarine Airport, but it didn't matter that she was late. The flight from London was late too, late enough for her to still have at least half an hour to kill. Having just swallowed a hurried breakfast at her parents' home in Hawthorn, Chris was not ready for more coffee yet, so she went up to the observation deck to await the plane's arrival.

And Adrian Gilmore.

She was nervous. Meeting Adrian like this was the last thing she wanted to do. If she'd known she would have to see him again, she would have thought twice about accepting the locum position in Mount William.

And yet she couldn't help being curious about him. Would he have changed much in eight years? she wondered. Of course they both must have changed a good deal. Although it was hard to recall his face clearly, she didn't doubt that she would recognise him. He was a big man with broad shoulders and muscular arms and legs—a rugby-player's physique, she'd always thought, although he didn't actually play the game. He had dark brown unruly hair that topped a square-jawed face with chiselled nose and a firm mouth. His eyes had a piercing quality as though at a glance he could diagnose all your ills and see into your soul as well. It was strange how she could remember details about him, yet his whole face was somehow elusive.

Then, suddenly, treacherously, she was remembering how it had felt to be held in his arms, the roughly affectionate bear-hug he had always greeted her with, catching her unawares sometimes in empty lifts and corridors and gowning rooms . . . and then, by contrast, she was remembering the languorous caresses

5

he had loved her with . . . She had always felt so safe in Adrian's arms, so cared for . . .

Chris's lissome body gave a little shudder as long-forgotten sensations disturbed her composure and brought a burning colour to her cheeks. She mustn't allow memories like that, painful or otherwise, to play any part in the next few months. If only she'd known from the start that he would be coming home! She couldn't blame Janet. His mother hadn't expected him either.

Chris leaned against the railing a little apart from the sprinkling of other people waiting for planes to arrive and take off. Shreds of mist were still rising from the bush and paddocks beyond the runways and a strong, chilly breeze buffeted her. But the sky would clear to a fine day once the mist had gone. A jumbo taxied out to the main runway and a few moments later was airborne. A couple of 727s from the interstate terminal followed it, then an airbus. Chris felt a pang of impatience. She couldn't wait to be jetting off again herself, back to Africa. A year, the tropical diseases specialist had advised her. She must not go back too soon.

'Why go back at all, Christine?' he mother had pleaded anxiously. 'You could get a good job here in Melbourne, I'm sure.' She sighed. 'The trouble is, you're too self-effacing. You should push yourself forward more.'

Chris smiled and shrugged. She wasn't interested in pushing herself forward. She was only interested in doing her job which, in recent years, had been a demanding one in a clinic in a drought-racked, famine-scourged area of Mali, one of the African countries where death and deprivation were as familiar as the rising and setting of the sun.

She said simply, 'There's so much to do out there . . .'

Concern for her daughter's health made Ellen persist. 'You've done your bit, surely?'

Again Chris shrugged. 'One has never "done one's bit", Mum,' she said quietly. 'Besides, I've got Africa in my blood!'

'And it makes you ill!'

Chris curbed her impatience because she understood her mother's concern and appreciated it. 'I just happened to get a rather virulent tropical fever,' she said, 'and because I'd been working extra hard, without a break, it hit me harder than it should have done. It was just one of those things.'

Her mother gave up arguing with her, knowing it was useless. Chris always did what she wanted to do. 'But, Chris, you know you'll overwork again.'

'No, I won't. If I crack up again, the Foundation won't give me another chance. I'll have to take care.'

Her mother said impetuously, 'Christine dear, I do wish you could meet some nice man and settle down . . .' She clipped off the involuntary words. Her daughter's face had closed up as it always did at the mention of marriage. Ellen Hart sighed. Dedication was one thing, but . . .

A plane came in to land and Chris squinted at it against the dazzling sunlight. She tensed, but it was only a local flight. She relaxed again and stared into the distance. Becoming ill herself had been unexpected and being forced to leave Africa for a whole year had been a bitter pill to swallow, even though she knew that the medical foundation she worked for would be only too delighted to have her back when she was ready. Providing of course that she passed a rigorous medical.

So, sensibly, she was trying to curb her impatience and the temptation to try and return too soon. As soon as she was well enough to work, because she couldn't stand doing nothing, she had found employment as a locum in the South City General Hospital in Melbourne where, ironically, nine years ago she had met Adrian Gilmore.

This time she had met Adrian's father, who had been admitted for heart surgery. It had been a shock to discover who the patient was, a coincidence that evoked both happy and painful memories. Andrew Gilmore,

however, had been delighted to find, in the course of
conversation, that she knew his son.

So far as Chris could tell, he knew nothing at all of
their former close relationship, the relationship she
should never have allowed to develop. She did not tell
him now, of course, that she and Adrian had been more
than just colleagues in the same hospital and that she
had even deceived herself that they would marry, until
Adrian had quite unwittingly proved to her how
unthinkable that was.

She'd been an intern when she'd met Adrian Gilmore,
and he a registrar. She had imagined him continuing a
hospital career and so she was surprised to learn that he
had joined his father in general practice back in his
home town, Mount William.

Now, with seeing him again nerve-rackingly
imminent, feelings she had long suppressed, surfaced
suddenly and brought a tightness to her chest as she
remembered that year of happiness unbounded when
she, a newly qualified doctor, had fallen hopelessly in
love with Adrian, and how it had ended . . .

Before he was discharged, Dr Gilmore had invited her
to act as locum at the Banksia Park Medical Centre in
Mount William until he was fit enough to return to
work himself. She had hesitated at first, but having
learnt in conversation with him that Adrian was
overseas on a trip that was part holiday and part
attending medical conferences in various countries and
was not expected back for several months, she had let
herself be persuaded. The offer was just what she
needed, a chance to get out of the city with its clamour
and pollution which she hated, and living in the country
might temper her impatience to get back to Mali. She
would be gone again before Adrian returned. Although
a part of her longed to see him again, she knew that
would be foolish, and if she'd thought there was the
least chance she would, she would never have accepted
Andrew Gilmore's offer.

Although Chris had grown up in Melbourne, she had

never been to Mount William. The medium-sized country town in the Central Highlands had proved a pleasant surprise when she had driven up to visit the Gilmores. The year would pass much more quickly for her there, she'd decided.

The town had immediately appealed to her with its tree-lined streets and original colonial buildings, many of which had been restored. Mount William was a former gold-mining town and had once been a prosperous centre, but it had gone into decline when the gold ran out at the turn of the century.

In recent times it had enjoyed a revival as a tourist centre for the increasingly popular Grampians mountains. There was also some decentralised light industry in the town as well as a thriving craft community of weavers, potters and other creative artists. Recently too one of the old goldmines had been re-opened as the rising price of gold on world markets had made operating it again economic. Dr Gilmore had also told Chris that a new tertiary educational institution was planned for Mount William. The town was growing rapidly.

Chris's enthusiasm for a few months in the country, however, had been dashed when Janet Gilmore had telephoned her only a couple of days ago to tell her that Adrian was coming home early and to ask her if she would mind meeting him.

'He'll be arriving on Saturday morning,' Janet said, 'and I thought, as you're coming up on Saturday . . .'

Chris caught her breath. 'But I thought he wouldn't be back for several months.' Her mouth was dry and her heart pounded. Janet had no inkling, of course, that Chris wanted to avoid her son. Chris hoped she hadn't betrayed her dismay and was glad Janet could not see her face. What a fool she'd been to take on this job. Self-indulgent wallowing in memories, which she admitted to herself she was bound to do living where Adrian normally was, and which she'd been unable to resist, was one thing. Actually seeing Adrian again was another.

Janet, unaware of her panic, said, 'We told him there was no need to cut his trip short, that Andrew was recovering well, but after he'd thought it over, he phoned back and insisted he was coming home.' She sounded glad nonetheless.

Adrian had been unreachable at the time of his father's operation and for a few weeks afterwards, apparently, so he had only just learned of it.

Janet Gilmore went on, 'There's no stopping Adrian when he decides to do something. I told him we had a locum coming up to help out at the clinic while his father's out of action, but it didn't make any difference.' She laughed in her vivacious way. 'I didn't tell him who you were! I just said it was someone he used to know from his South City General days and that it would be a very pleasant surprise! How nice it will be for you and Adrian to meet again after all!'

Chris tried to sound pleased, while wondering how Adrian might have reacted if his mother had told him who the new locum was. Would he perhaps have decided against rushing home in a hurry? After all, there had been some bitter words between them . . .

'I know you'll be loaded up,' Janet apologised, 'but I don't expect he'll have much luggage. Adrian always travels light. He once hitch-hiked halfway round the world with a bar of chocolate and a toothbrush!'

Chris had smiled to herself at that. He'd told her all about the trip, which had taken place long before she'd met him, in his medical student days.

A glint of sunlight on silver dragged her eyes from the reminiscent distance to the present foreground. A plane was gliding down out of the blue, almost cloudless sky, and Chris knew instinctively even before she recognised the jumbo's big-fish shape and the insignia on the tail that this was Adrian's flight arriving.

She watched the plane land and taxi towards the terminal, her heart fluttering nervously as she pictured Adrian collecting his belongings, unaware of the shock in store for him. There might be a little awkwardness between them, she supposed, but surely after all this time . . .

She waited until the plane had docked in one of the bays and then ran down the stairs to the Arrivals area. A number was up on the board, she noticed. It was the flight she was waiting for.

Slowly the passengers trickled through Immigration and Customs. Chris scanned them tensely. There seemed to be an inordinate number of tall, dark-haired men travelling alone. Several times her heart jumped as she caught sight of someone she was sure was Adrian, only to be disappointed when a stranger's face was turned towards her.

Finally, he came through the barrier. He did not spot Chris immediately and she stood transfixed, all feeling suddenly drained from her body, her mind numbed. It was like seeing a stranger, and yet Adrian wasn't strange. A wild impulse to run into his arms rose up with frightening intensity, only to be overwhelmed by a surge of the innate shyness that any stranger would have evoked in her.

He paused, glancing round, a slight frown on his broad high forehead which supported the thatch of unruly brown hair. There was a faint shadow of beard on his cheeks and chin, emphasising the cleft in it. He looked weary. He put down his suitcase and scratched his temple, a familiar gesture that made Chris's heart lurch again. He must be intrigued to know who was meeting him. For another moment or two, Chris's feet refused to move. She needed those few seconds to compose herself. She hadn't expected seeing Adrian again to hit her with quite such an impact. She wished fervently that she'd never agreed to go to Mount William to work. But it was too late to get out of it now. She would never be able to think of an excuse plausible enough. Perhaps, when he saw for himself that his father was fine, he would resume his trip, she thought with wild hope.

Woodenly, she began to walk towards him, conscious that this was only the beginning of the ordeal.

She was almost at his side when the unexpected happened. A slim blonde woman clattered past her across the tiles on slender heels. To Chris's astonishment, the blonde ran straight up to Adrian, arms open wide, and gathered the weary and evidently astonished traveller into them.

Chris, a few feet away, having halted, nonplussed, caught a whiff of expensive perfume.

'Adrian darling!' the woman exclaimed, planting a kiss on his mouth. 'I thought you weren't coming back for months!'

With the tightness in her chest increasing, Chris watched as Adrian's arms clasped the woman and he smiled into the pretty pouting face that he obviously knew well.

'Deb! What are you doing here? I thought I was being met by someone from . . .'

'Coincidence, darling! I didn't even know you were coming back,' she cried delightedly, but with underlying reproach, Chris thought. 'Janet never said . . .'

'Mother didn't know herself until three days ago,' said Adrian. 'I decided to come back when she told me about Dad. But Mother said the new locum would meet me.' He frowned, puzzled. 'She said it was someone I know . . .' He broke off and glanced around. Inevitably this time his gaze met Chris's and her stomach contracted as the dark brown eyes flashed first recognition, then incredulity, before she found it necessary to avert her eyes. She marched forward, since there was nothing else she could do. She called up a welcoming smile, but it wavered a little on her lips.

'Hello, Adrian!' she forced herself to say brightly, assuming a nonchalance she did not feel and she was certain did not deceive him. It was impossible to untangle her feelings at that moment, so she firmly pushed the lid on them and prepared to skid along on the surface for as long as she needed to.

'Chris!' he exclaimed. 'Am I seeing things?'

His stunned expression helped her to smile. 'No! I'm real!'

He clasped her hand. 'Well, I'll be . . . How . . .?' He was practically speechless. He had never dreamed that his father's new locum would be Chris Hart. *Chris Hart!* His mind still shouted the name incredulously as he took in the slight frame, the glossy black hair which hugged her head like a shining helmet above delicately scrolled ears. It tumbled in a wayward fringe over her forehead, brushing the edge of her straight black brows that were not too sharply defined by plucking. Before, she'd had longer hair which she'd often worn in a thick plait off duty, he remembered, but coiled into a smooth chignon when on duty, and which, when loose, had run like silk through his fingers . . .

He looked searchingly into the clear grey eyes that she now turned to him again after that first somewhat embarrassed moment. Between them her straight nose with slightly flaring nostrils might have given a sternness to her features, but a full mobile mouth softened them, a mouth, Adrian thought waywardly, that still invited kissing.

And, my God, I still want to! he realised with a hunger in the pit of his stomach that he'd thought long since rubbed out. She was still the same Chris, just more mature, more womanly now. Her hair was different, and she was surely smaller, slimmer, more waif-like than ever, but she was still the Chris Hart he had known—and loved.

Was she the 'old friend' his mother had meant or was she here by coincidence too, like Deborah? When his mother had said the new locum had been working in Africa and had been ill, he'd automatically thought of some male colleague. Of course his mother was innocent of the knowledge of what Chris had once meant to him.

He said, in what sounded to his ears like a strangled tone, 'Are you the new locum? You were one of the doctors who attended Dad at the hospital?'

Chris, floundering in a whirlpool of emotion, nodded, then found her voice. 'Yes, I was working there part-time for a while, and I was in the Cardiac Unit. I'm sorry if it's a bit of a shock, but your mother wanted to surprise you.' She didn't want him to think not telling him who was meeting him had been her idea. She was aware of the blonde woman eyeing her curiously and a little warily.

Adrian's arm was still loosely around the blonde, but he now let it fall and for a moment Chris thought he was going to envelop her in a familiar bear-hug, but he didn't. He just stood there nonplussed, and she began to feel sorry for him. Mrs Gilmore should have prepared him.

The blonde turned her face up to Adrian's and tugged at his sleeve. She smiled expectantly as she fluttered her lashes. 'What's all this about, Adrian? Aren't you going to introduce us?'

He glanced at her, then at Chris. 'Oh—yes, of course, I'm sorry. This is Dr Hart—Chris and I worked together years ago at South City General Hospital. She met Dad while he was in hospital recently and he offered her a locum job at Mount William. Right, Chris?'

Chris nodded, and smiled ruefully. 'I was moaning about hating working in the city and he said why didn't I try a few months' stint in the country.'

'Chris, this is Deborah Leigh,' Adrian went on. 'She lives in Mount William. She's a potter.'

The two women acknowledged each other briefly, and Chris was clearly informed by Deborah's frank gaze that she had first claim on Adrian. Chris would have liked to have assured her that she had nothing to fear from her, but she could hardly do that.

Adrian turned to Deborah. 'What are you doing here?'

Deborah tucked her arm proprietorially through his. 'I came to see a friend off. I've been staying in Melbourne for a few days, so I haven't seen Janet lately, or I'm sure she would have told me you were coming back and asked me to meet you.'

Adrian was still trying to take in the reality that Chris was standing there, small and neat in her smart tweed suit and fashionable shoes. Had she really been slogging in a clinic in some Godforsaken outpost in Africa, battling famine and disease? No wonder she had succumbed in the end herself. A wave of irrational outrage welled up in him at the thought of it.

Chris was saying in her soft, slightly husky voice, 'As I'm travelling up today, your mother asked me if I'd mind driving you home. She doesn't like leaving your father and it seemed silly for you to hire a car when I could easily meet you.'

Adrian nodded. 'It was good of you—especially as you're probably loaded up.'

'Not really . . .'

Deborah put in, 'Well, there's no need to inconveniece Dr Hart, Adrian. There's plenty of room in my car. I can take you home. I'm going straight back to Mount William.' She smoothed the collar of his jacket. 'Poor darling, you must be worn out. You flew straight from London?'

'Yes, I had the chance of a cancellation, so naturally I took it. Dad . . .' His eyes returned to Chris. 'How is he?'

Chris was glad she could reassure him. 'He's fine, Adrian. You know he had Mr Townshend.'

'Yes, Mother told me. I was glad of that.' Bryce Townshend was one of Australia's finest heart surgeons.

'He's come through it very well. In fact your mother will have a hard time keeping him away from the practice, I'm sure. It was she who was most anxious to have a locum in, especially as you were away too, and the last one had recently left.'

Adrian said, 'That's what was worrying me too. I know my father! He'll try to go back to work too soon. He always puts the patients first.'

And always so did you, Chris thought.

Deborah began to sound impatient. 'Well, don't let's stand around here. Poor Adrian must be ready to drop. Come along, let's go.' She seemed to have taken it for granted that Adrian would go with her now. Chris saw no reason to argue, but she was annoyed with herself for the involuntary disappointment she felt, rather than relief.

'I'll be a late lunch for everyone as it is,' Deborah pressed, tapping her wristwatch.

Adrian considered his dilemma—which woman should he let drive him home? Did Chris really want to? He regarded her thoughtfully. How much did what had happened eight years ago mean to her now? Would she have taken the job at Mount William if she'd known he was coming home?

He said, trying to make light of the situation, 'Look, girls, I'm enormously flattered having both of you offering me a lift! Shall we toss a coin or will you duel?'

Deborah looked unamused at his facetiousness, but Chris caught his eye and grinned. She decided to resolve it for him.

'I'm sure you'll be more comfortable in Deborah's car, Adrian,' she said firmly. She guessed that Deborah's vehicle would be roomier and smarter than the rather battered second-hand Honda she had bought to drive while in Australia.

Adrian heard her words with an involuntary shaft of disappointment that surprised him. She was relieved to offload him. He ought to feel relieved too, he supposed, but all he felt was total confusion. It was all too unexpected and his brain was befuddled by jet-lag. All he wanted to do was to get hime, take a long hot shower, clean his teeth and shave, then sleep the clock round. It wasn't just the effect of the long flight; he'd had a hectic couple of days beforehand with next to no sleep.

'Well, if that's settled . . .' Deborah, with evident satisfaction, began to walk away.

Adrian picked up his luggage and followed with Chris

at his side. 'Sorry about this,' he muttered. 'It was good of you to come . . .'

'There's no need to apologise,' said Chris, not looking at him.

Deborah called from the exit, 'Wait here, Adrian, and I'll bring the car around.'

Chris, out of politeness, waited with him. During those few moments neither spoke, but they exchanged one rueful, slightly embarrassed glance before Deborah arrived. As Chris had expected, Deborah's car was more luxurious than hers. The sleek blue Mazda afforded much more room for Adrian's long legs, she noticed.

He stowed his luggage in the boot, and Chris said, 'Well, I'll be off now. See you in Mount William. Will you be at the clinic on Monday morning?'

Adrian detained her. 'Wait! You're coming for lunch today, aren't you? I mean . . .'

Chris would have stayed for lunch with the Gilmores if she had driven Adrian home. Now she decided she would rather get out of it. 'It'll be late, Adrian, and really, now I'd rather get settled into my place. Janet said she'd stocked the fridge for me, so I won't starve. Your mother really has been very kind.'

He seemed disappointed. 'But won't she be expecting you for lunch?'

'Apologise for me, please,' Chris said, and with an involuntary touch of acid, unlike her, added, 'I'm sure Deborah will be happy to take my place.'

Adrian frowned, but said nothing. Deborah was urging them to get moving. 'We can't park here all day,' she said. 'Taxis will start complaining.'

Chris said goodbye and walked quickly away. Out of the corner of her eye, she saw the Mazda proceed smoothly away from the terminal. Gritting her teeth, she walked to her own car. She was committed now and couldn't go back on her commitment. What would the next few months bring? Would it be easy working with Adrian, or some kind of hell?

It ought to be easy, she told herself firmly as she slid behind the Honda's wheel. She and Adrian would be no more than a part of a team, just a couple of old friends who'd met up again. The past would simply not come into it. That could only happen if she let it, and she certainly wouldn't do that. She didn't think Adrian would want to bring it up either.

# CHAPTER TWO

ADRIAN listened absently to Deborah's chatter as the Mazda sped up the Western Highway. He murmured a reply here and there which seemed to satisfy her, although it was hardly conversational. Deborah, as usual, was more interested in telling him about herself and her doings than enquiring about his trip, which for once he was thankful for. His thoughts drifted inevitably to Chris Hart.

He was still stunned at the impact seeing her again had made on him, and annoyed that he'd been hijacked by Deborah. Although perhaps the atmosphere might have been strained between them if Chris had driven him. No, surely not. Eight years was a long time—long enough to forget—only he hadn't forgotten.

Eventually Deborah's rather monotonous tone sent him off to sleep as he slid further into the luxurious upholstery. Noticing it, Deborah smiled fondly and put it down to jet-lag. Her expression was triumph at having brought off a coup. Something instinctive warned her to beware of Chris. The new locum had the kind of intriguing good looks that would be very attractive to a man. No doubt she would learn more about her over lunch. Deborah has already assumed she would be invited to lunch with the Gilmores. Deborah frowned impatiently. If only Adrian would make up his mind to settle down . . . she wasn't getting any younger either . . .

Chris drove at a steady speed up the Western Highway, at, she guessed, some little distance behind the others as she'd had a spot of bother finding her way after leaving the airport. She felt angry with herself, for getting sick. If she hadn't fallen ill none of this would be happening. She smiled a little ruefully at the futility of

19

the thought. One couldn't help getting sick, but for doctors to become ill always seemed somehow to reflect on their competency. She remembered her mother saying, 'And you a doctor too!' as though there ought to be magic immunity from disease for medicos, or else she was being blamed for not taking proper care of herself.

Perhaps she hadn't, she reflected honestly. But it was difficult to live as you were accustomed to out there, to worry about yourself when there was so much misery around you. The contrast to life in suburban Australia was so stark, even a meagre existence could seem like an indulgence. She'd been in a pretty bad way when she'd come home, thin to the point of emaciation, they'd said, when she'd been admitted to hospital. But no one here knew what real emaciation was like, what the bones of small children looked like seen through a parchment skin that seemed about to split and fall off like an insect's pupal case. Only there was no beautiful body underneath, only a pathetic skeleton.

Expertly, Chris swung the Honda round the wide curves in the road and looked with pleasure at the soft green rolling countryside, so different from the desert wastes and sparse scrub country she had become accustomed to, driving out in jeeps with the medical team to remote villages or camps.

Here, at winter's end, the pastures were bright green and the wheat was sprouting vigorously. Black and white cows gave the landscape a sentimental picture-book quality, until now and then she glimpsed long, windowless sheds, their roofs glinting in the sunlight, which reminded her that they probably housed hens in battery cages or pigs tethered in narrow pens. You didn't often see pigs and chickens in the fields nowadays. They never saw the sun. Economics had changed all that, and the realities of factory farming were carefully hidden from public scrutiny. Maybe even the placid cows would disappear behind locked doors in time too. Chris took a deep breath, disturbed as always by the thought of human inhumanity to other animals.

Her attention was soon dragged to contemplation of a different kind of cruelty. Alongside the road, the passing of each car stirred innumerable heaps of feathers, mostly the black and white of magpies and peewits, the glossy jet black of ravens, sometimes the soft pink and grey of galahs, a gruesome harvest from speeding vehicles. Birds died in thousands every year on country roads, especially the young, recently fledged and inexperienced, in spring.

It was always the young who suffered most, she thought. The babies and young children of Mali with their large grape-black eyes and their malnutrition stares, their distended bellies, flashed on to her inward eye and she longed to be back there. Perhaps it was because she would never have children of her own that she cared so much, she sometimes thought.

'Oh, come on, Christine, you're being much too solemn for such a fine day!' she chided herself as she reached the outskirts of Ballarat. 'You're too introspective, that's your trouble.'

She lingered a while in Ballarat, stopping for coffee, then driving around the town and taking time to admire the brilliant flowerbeds in the median strips, the old colonial buildings and the magnificent gardens which edged the lake. Ballarat was a cold spot in winter, but on a fine day like today, very pleasant. She must pay a visit to Sovereign Hill again, she reminded herself. The recreated old goldmining town had always fascinated her and there were bound to have been additions since she had last been there.

There would be plenty to occupy her free time, she thought, as she finally left the town behind her and drove along the magnificent memorial avenue of trees which had been planted to commemorate the dead of World War I. Mount William was ideally situated for exploring in all directions, and particularly handy to the Grampians which she had never visited. She would go bushwalking as often as she could, she decided eagerly. It would help to make her really fit. The time would pass quickly and it should be easy not to see too much of Adrian.

The owners of the house she was renting were abroad for a year and she'd secured a four-month lease on it, which was about how long she expected to stay in Mount William—just until Christmas. Janet Gilmore had found the house for her, and when she had driven up to inspect it, Chris had been enchanted with the old weatherboard house with its iron-lace festooned verandah, fancy cornices and open fireplaces.

The garden was large and tangled, with a huge walnut tree at the back and a dozen different varieties of acacias in both front and back. Some of the wattles were flowering now and the blaze of gold had made the house seem sunny even on the dull dreary day when she had viewed it. Fortunately it was being let fully furnished, which suited Chris perfectly.

She was so engrossed in her thoughts that she nearly missed the exit road, which was a shorter route to Mount William than going through Ararat. This road was narrower and winding, but it was more picturesque and carried less traffic. Chris was in no great hurry now, so she slowed down to enjoy the tranquil undulating countryside under the vivid blue sky. The hills, which were closer now, kept changing colour from deep blue to purple as the sailing-ship clouds passed across the sun, and sometimes there were patches of gold as sunlight slanted through cloud. Mount William, from which the town took its name, stood out prominently amid the jagged ridges of sandstone.

There were things about African scenery that sometimes reminded Chris of Australia, especially stands of gum trees, which caused her an occasional nostalgic pang. But this Victorian countryside was more like England or Wales, picturesque now and very green. This wasn't the sunburnt country, the wide brown land of Dorothy MacKellar's famous poem—at least not in winter and spring—although there were certainly some 'rugged mountain ranges' in the Grampians. And now and then a windmill and a typical homestead to remind the traveller that this was indeed Australia.

Cows had given way to sheep in most of the paddocks and on the edges of dams stately herons and pure white cattle egrets paraded, while pelicans patrolled the water in small flotillas. Little black and white chats darted off the fence wires from time to time and nankeen kestrels hovered over the fields while ravens and magpies scavenged for insects in the furrows of ploughed fields.

When Chris tooted a loud warning, a flock of pink and grey galahs rose from the roadside. Chris automatically slackened speed, and as she did so, there was a loud prolonged blast on a car horn from close behind her. She had been too busy watching birds to be aware of its approach. As a blue utility screamed past her, she glimpsed a youth at the wheel. He was driving one-handed, his other hand gripping the roof, elbow resting on the window-ledge. The vehicle wobbled dangerously as it swept past.

'Fool! Idiot!' Chris shouted ineffectually as the Honda almost swerved out of control in the buffeting wind the speeding vehicle created. 'That's the way to kill yourself! And someone else if you aren't careful!'

The ute roared heedlessly on and vanished around a bend. As Chris also negotiated the curve which swooped into a deep depression with a culvert at the bottom, she gasped in horror. The road narrowed slightly at the culvert and approaching it at the same time as the ute was a cyclist. Chris's yell was involuntary and futile. She saw the cyclist fly into the air and over the neat white railing of the bridge, while the ute sped on without stopping.

When Chris reached the spot, her heart was in her mouth, the bicycle was the first thing she saw, halfway down the incline to the creek, one wheel still spinning. The cyclist, she saw, sick with dismay, was sprawled in the paddock, having been tossed right over the wire fence.

'You criminal!' she yelled after the vanished utility truck.

She ran down the incline and squeezed through the fence. The victim of the hit-and-run driver was lying ominously still. Blood was oozing from a flesh wound in his cheek, but he was still wearing his helmet.

Chris examined him and heaved a sigh of relief when she felt the fluttering pulse under her fingers. His facial wound was not serious, but she was afraid he might have sustained internal injuries besides the obvious broken leg. She knew she would be unable to move the boy unaided. Although probably only about fourteen, he was a big lad and too heavy for her to shift. There was always the danger of aggravating a spinal injury if she tried. She must get help.

It was an isolated spot. There was no farmhouse in view and the ute was the only vehicle she had seen so far. She could only hope someone else would come along before she would have to decide to go for help herself. Meanwhile, she fetched her medical bag and a couple of rugs, and at the same time angled her car across the road so that a vehicle from either direction would have to stop.

She staunched the blood from the boy's head injury, and as she was applying a dressing, he came round briefly.

'My leg . . .' he groaned. 'What happened?'

'Lie still,' Chris urged. 'You're all right. Help's coming, and I'm a doctor. But you must lie still. You might injure yourself more if you move.'

As he squeezed her hand, a spasm of pain crossed his youthful features. 'Who—are—you?'

'I'm Dr Hart,' she said. 'Don't worry, we'll soon have you in hospital. You were knocked off your bike and you've broken your leg. But you'll be all right.'

He looked at her with a fleeting smile of relief and gratitude, then his expression became anxious again. 'My bike . . . Dad'll kill me!' His gaze wavered and he promptly passed out again.

Chris regarded him for a moment indecisively. She needed an ambulance, which meant either stopping a passing motorist or going to the nearest phone herself. She didn't want to leave the boy, but if someone didn't come she would have to.

Fortunately, luck was with her and the cyclist. Five minutes later as she was climbing back up the incline, ready to go for help herself, she heard a vehicle approaching. As she reached the road, a camper-van braked sharply near her car and a man leapt out.

'Hey, what's happened? Is it an accident? Are you all right?' He ran anxiously to her side and three other young people piled out of the camper-van.

'I'm all right—but there's a young boy hurt,' Chris told them, and explained why she'd left her car at such a crazy angle. 'Could you go to the nearest phone and call an ambulance?' she finished. 'The boy must be hospitalised as quickly as possible.'

The two men and two girls were eager to help. One of the girls said, 'Why don't we take him? We could put one of the beds down in the van. That'd be quicker.'

The others murmured agreement. Chris hesitated for a moment, however, uneasy about carrying the boy up the steep incline without a proper stretcher. One of the men seemed to read her thought.

'We've got a camp-bed we can use as a stretcher,' he said, adding, 'Is his back hurt?'

'I don't know,' said Chris. 'We'll have to be very careful.' She looked them over. They were sensible young people. They would do exactly as she told them.

A few moments later, under her supervision, the two men carried the unconscious boy on the camp-bed up to the camper-van which the girls had meanwhile made ready.

'Gee, he's only a kid!' exclaimed one of them, adding angrily, 'I hope they catch the creep that did it.'

Chris went in the camper-van with the patient, leaving one of the campers to drive her car. They were only a few kilometres from the town so were soon in the hospital yard. Chris rushed in for help and orderlies dashed back with her to transfer the injured boy to the Casualty Department.

When Chris went out to thank the campers and ask for

their names, she found to her disappointment that they had gone. Only the Honda stood waiting for her. Her next task was to report the accident to the police. By the time she had done that and had given them as clear a description of the hit-and-run vehicle and its driver as she could, the afternoon was half gone. Although it was long past lunchtime, she wasn't hungry.

She drove away from the hospital and along the wide quiet streets to her rented house, wanting no more now than to have a cup of tea and a rest. It had been a somewhat traumatic morning, one way and another.

As she walked up to the front door, she heard the telephone ringing, but by the time she had let herself in the caller had rung off.

'Probably Janet,' she thought. 'Or Mum checking I've arrived safely.' She decided she needed a cup of tea before she called either of them, so she went into the kitchen and switched on the kettle. She was touched by how welcoming Janet Gilmore has made the house. The fridge was well stocked, so were the pantry cupboards and there were fresh flowers in a vase on the windowsill.

Chris went out to the car and carried in the first load of gear. She dumped everything in a heap in the living-room. She would sort it out later. The kettle boiled and she made a pot of tea, then went out to bring in the rest of her belongings while it was drawing.

She was bending over the boot when a car drew up right behind her and a man jumped out. 'Chris!'

Chris straightened and turned around. Adrian strode across to her, looking taller and broader somehow than he had this morning. He looked steadily into her face, his expression still showing amazement at her being there.

'We've been phoning all afternoon,' he said. 'We thought you must have had an accident. When I checked with the hospital just now, in case you were there, they told me about the hit-and-run. I just missed you at the police station.' He sounded breathless, as though he'd been running all over town looking for her. He didn't tell her how relieved he'd been to know she hadn't been hurt.

Chris said stiffly, 'I'm sorry. I didn't expect anyone to be worried about me.'

'My mother was furious with me for abandoning you after you'd gone to the trouble of meeting me. She said I should have insisted you come to lunch. She was on the phone to make amends straight away, but couldn't raise you.'

'I'm sorry . . .'

'What happened?'

Chris told him and almost invited him in for a cup of tea, but she checked the impulse.

He rested a hand on her shoulder. 'Well you're off to a good start! You'll be the talk of the town by tomorrow!'

'I hope not!' she exclaimed in dismay, adding urgently, 'How's the boy? Did they tell you anything at the hospital?'

'Only that he's got a broken leg and broken ribs, but no obvious spinal or internal injuries, thank goodness. He was lucky. The bank must have been soft. His name's John Portman, by the way. He's a patient of mine as it happens. Steady young lad. It's a shame.'

'I'm glad his injuries aren't so serious,' said Chris.

'It was lucky you were right behind him and saw it happen!' Adrian said. 'He could have lain there for hours before he was found. And then it might have been a different story.'

For a moment after he had spoken, they looked at each other in silence. Chris flinched as a sudden tide of memories washed over her, some happy, some painful. She felt, uncannily, that they momentarily meshed with his and knew he was remembering too.

'I'll give you a hand with that,' he offered abruptly, breaking the silence. He reached for her suitcase which she had only half dragged out of the boot. He felt unreal, almost as though the intervening years had not happened. He was surprised to find she was still single and wondered if she was as surprised to find that he was too.

Chris dragged her eyes from his face. 'It's all right, thanks, there isn't much more . . .'

But he was carrying the case down the path to the verandah where he set it down. Chris followed with her arms full of clothing. She said, 'I'm sorry your mother was anxious. The phone was ringing when I arrived but it stopped before I could get to it. I thought it might be her and I intended ringing later. Please tell her I'll . . .'

'Yes—yes, I'd better go and set her mind at rest,' he said, then added, 'You'll come to dinner, won't you?'

Chris drew in a deep breath. 'Thank you, Adrian, but I'd really rather just settle in here tonight. It's kind of your mother, but . . .' She added quickly, 'And as you've only just arrived home . . .'

Adrian smiled. 'All right. But you'd better promise to come for lunch tomorrow. On reflection, that's probably a much better idea. I might be more lively company by then!'

Chris managed to laugh. 'Jet-lag is a bind, isn't it? And there's no cure for it yet. It's strange how it hits some people harder than others.'

Her clear grey eyes were as beautiful as he remembered, Adrian thought, but looked larger in her almost gaunt face and there were scars in them now, emotional scars. Caused by her work, he wondered, or by someone who had hurt her? Had there been someone else? He had never known for sure. A wave of anger against a possible unknown man who might have jilted her, caught him by surprise.

'Will you come to lunch tomorrow?' he pressed.

'Yes, thank you, that would be nice. What time? About twelve?'

'Earlier if you can—in time for a sherry!' He smiled, and wanted suddenly to smooth the fine lines fanning out from her eyes and run his fingers through that silky dark hair.

He went reluctantly back to his car and Chris watched as he executed an expert U-turn in the wide street. He gave her a brief wave and was gone. Chris carried her bundle into the house and went back to lock her car. Then she sat down to enjoy her cup of tea. It had stood long enough to be very strong and she felt she needed that.

# CHAPTER THREE

WHEN Chris woke on Sunday morning, the conviction that she should never have risked accepting the job at Mount William was stronger than ever. She ought to have considered the possibility that Adrian would come home when he learned about his father's illness, she told herself now, glooming over her morning cup of tea. Wasn't it what she would have wanted to do herself in the same circumstances?

Chris sighed. She wished she didn't have to front up at the Gilmores' for lunch today, but Janet would think her rather strange if she made some excuse.

'I've got to get used to seeing him,' she said aloud, pacing the kitchen while she waited for the toast to pop up. 'I just mustn't let my feelings get involved again, that's all.'

The knowledge that her feelings were vulnerable was galling. She'd believed she'd put Adrian Gilmore right out of her mind and heart a long time ago, but seeing him yesterday had shown her how wrong she had been. It had all come back so vividly that her dreams had been full of Adrian last night and she had woken several times imagining his arms around her, only to be overwhelmed by bleak disappointment when she found that hers clasped only the tangled bedclothes.

'If only he were married,' she thought, 'it might be easier.'

It had surprised her to find that he was not. So often in the past she had thought of him, wistfully, with a wife and growing children.

After breakfast, Chris set about distributing her belongings and organising the kitchen the way she wanted it. Time flew and she had to hurry in the end to change out of her old jeans and sweater into something a little

29

more respectable for lunch at the Gilmores'. She teamed claret-coloured cords with a white skivvy. A heavy-knit cardigan that matched the cords gave the impression of a little more substance to her slender frame.

The Gilmores' house was on the edge of town and set in a large natural bush garden. It was a low ranch-style building, placed well back from the street and approached by a driveway lined with mature gum trees. On all sides there were views across farmland towards the mountains, which seemed very close today, and intensely blue.

Andrew Gilmore's two black and white cocker spaniels rushed out to greet her, closely followed by Janet who was trying vainly to curb their ebullience.

'Down, Tess! Down, Dick!' she scolded, while Chris protested that she didn't mind their affectionate welcome.

Janet clasped her warmly as though she were a daughter, not just someone she had recently met. 'Chris, we were so worried about you yesterday. What a traumatic start for you!'

Chris brushed it aside. 'It's the kind of thing I'm supposed to be able to cope with!'

Janet led her into the house. 'How lucky it was for poor young John Portman that you saw what happened. I hope they catch that lunatic.'

'So do I,' agreed Chris with feeling. 'That boy could easily have been killed. It was a miracle he wasn't and didn't sustain any really serious injuries either.'

'And how are you settling in?' Janet asked as they went through the front door. 'I hope you found everything you needed.'

'Indeed I did,' Chris said. 'It was marvellous of you to stock up the cupboards, and you cleaned the place right through too, didn't you?'

Janet chuckled. 'Well, my cleaning woman did it, I have to confess. I used to do all my own housework, but the more I got tied up with local affairs, the less time I seemed to have and since I took on the organisation of the local Meals on Wheels, I've hardly had a spare minute. I'll have to be at home for a while, though, although Andrew insists he doesn't need me.'

'How is he?' Chris asked.

'Come and see for yourself.' Janet led the way to the living room where Andrew Gilmore was reading the weekend paper. Adrian was not there.

Andrew rose. 'Chris, my dear, how nice to see you at last. You gave us all a bit of a fright yesterday, but it seems you were being a Good Samaritan.'

Chris shrugged. 'How are you feeling now?'

'Fine, fine . . .' he said, eyebrows bristling a bit, and a twist of impatience in his smile. 'Straining at the leash,' he admitted with a laugh, 'but not for much longer, I hope.'

Janet said, 'I'm glad Adrian's home. At least he'll help me to keep you in order!'

Andrew threw up his hands in defeat and said, 'Forget about me. Sit down, Chris. A drink? Sherry?'

'Thank you.' Chris sank into an armchair. As she had the first time she'd visited, she felt instantly at home in the comfortable, slightly old-fashioned living room.

Janet excused herself to check on the dinner, saying as she left them, 'I'm afraid Adrian isn't awake yet. We shouldn't have stayed up so late last night talking.'

By the time she was ready to serve the meal, Adrian had still not emerged.

Andrew said, 'You'd better wake him, Janet.'

Chris put in quickly, 'No, leave him. Let him sleep. It's better to sleep off jet-lag in one go.' She forced a laugh. 'Tell him I forgave him!'

'He'll be very cross if I don't . . .' Janet said doubtfully.

'Nonsense. He'll be seeing more than enough of me,' Chris said, and hoped that if the colour seeping into her cheeks was noticeable, they would blame the sherry. Adrian might even be glad he'd missed her.

'Well . . .' Janet was still uncertain.

'Please don't disturb him on my account,' Chris insisted.

Janet gave in and they ate without Adrian. During lunch, Chris found herself being quizzed in more detail by Janet about her previous friendship with Adrian. It seemed that he had said very little about it, so she avoided going into detail and gave the impression that it had been a very casual relationship. It was obvious from what Janet said that she was more than a little anxious to see her son married and producing grandchildren, like the rest of her children.

'I keep telling Adrian he'll leave it too late!' Janet said, with a touch of exasperation. 'But he just shrugs and says we've got more than enough grandchildren around with Rachel's brood.'

Rachel was Adrian's sister whom Chris had already heard quite a bit about. She and her dentist husband lived in Ballarat and had five children, which included two sets of twins. There was also another sister living in Western Australia and one in Mildura, as well as two brothers, one in Sydney, the other in Brisbane. All except Adrian were married with families. Chris hoped Janet wasn't pinning any hopes on her as a matrimonial prospect for Adrian. She said, 'Maybe he's just not the marrying kind.'

'Not everyone sees domesticity as the ultimate bliss!' joked Andrew, winking at Chris.

Janet turned to him. 'Oh, you! You were falling over yourself to get married and raise a family, and you dote on your grandchildren.'

'And on your wife too, I'm sure!' put in Chris, laughing. Andrew was a wicked tease. There was a lot of him in Adrian.

Janet sighed. 'It just seems such a waste of a good man!'

'You're old-fashioned, believing everyone should get married,' said her husband. 'Some people prefer to dedicate themselves to their work. Look at Chris here. She's not married either. Marriage isn't the bottom line for everyone, my dear. We live in a different age now.'

Janet was unconvinced. 'Marriage is natural,' she said flatly, and frowning at Chris, 'And whatever you say, it's just as big a shame that a nice girl like you isn't married!'

Andrew made a helpless gesture. 'You'll never shift her, Chris, so be warned. Janet fancies herself as a matchmaker and she'll be doing her best to get you and Adrian to the altar if you're not careful. She's a very determined woman!'

Chris flinched, but managed a light-hearted reply. 'I think you might have more success, Janet, if you worked on Deborah Leigh. You'd be halfway there already, I'm sure.'

To her surprise Janet's lips pursed. She said stiffly, 'I've nothing against Deborah, but I don't think she would be right for Adrian. She's too arty for one thing.'

'I thought he seemed pretty fond of her,' Andrew said, stirring deliberately, Chris thought.

'Rubbish! Adrian only takes her out when she asks him to! She chases him, and men don't like being chased. If you ask me he went off on this trip partly because she was stifling him.'

Andrew sighed. 'I think Adrian is perfectly capable of organising his love-life without any help from you, nonetheless, my dear!'

Janet capitulated with a laugh, then said wistfully, 'I only want to see him happy, like all the others. I feel he may have been let down badly once and it's soured his attitude to marriage.'

Chris avoided her eyes and wished they would change the subject. Her feelings of guilt had been more sharply aroused than she cared to admit. Had her rejection of him really turned Adrian against marriage? She couldn't believe it. After all, people break off relationships all the time. It needn't necessarily have been because of her. He must have met any number of women after they'd broken up. Eight years was time enough for anything to have happened.

To her relief, Andrew did change the subject and they began to discuss a new development in the treatment of heart disease which was replacing the need for bypass surgery in certain cases.

Then the topic switched to wine, and the chardonnay they were drinking with dinner. Chris learned that Adrian owned a vineyard not far from Mount William and the wine was made from his grapes.

'It's certainly delicious,' Chris said, as Andrew replenished her glass. She went on with a laugh, 'Not that I'm a connoisseur. I just know what I like.'

Andrew nodded agreement. 'That's what matters.'

Janet put in, 'You must ask Adrian to take you out to Ravensbush some time.'

Chris made a non-committal reply. She expected that Adrian might not be terribly anxious to entertain her.

All through lunch, she was on tenterhooks expecting Adrian to appear at any minute, but he didn't. After lunch, Janet went to his room and came back to report that he was still dead to the world.

'He had a hectic week of conferences before he came home, don't forget,' Andrew reminded her. 'It's more than just jet-lag.'

As soon as she felt she could, Chris excused herself, saying she still had things to sort out and some letters to write and phone calls to make. Janet tried to persuade her to stay for the evening meal as well, but Chris wriggled out of the invitation because she did not want to get into the habit of spending too much time at the Gilmores'.

On Monday morning, Chris arrived early at the Banksia Park Medical Centre. She stood outside for a few moments, letting her eyes run over the attractive modern building in its garden setting, surrounded by large shady trees. It was opposite a park from which it had taken its name.

There had been two old weatherboard houses on the site, Janet had told her when she had taken her there on her previous visit. They had been demolished and the new surgery complex had been carefully sited so as to preserve as many of the old trees and existing garden as possible.

Chris drove into the car-park, a gravel area fenced with a low edging of split pine logs which divided it from the lawns and flower beds. The white-painted building had contrasting brown window frames and fascia boards and a green-tiled roof. It looked more like a motel, Chris thought.

She pushed open the double glass doors and entered the foyer, off which was situated a spacious and cheerfully decorated waiting room. One of the nurses was already behind the reception desk. It was Rose MacLeod, the Scots girl to whom Chris had chatted for a while on her first visit.

Rose looked up, and her rather serious features broke into a warm smile.

'Dr Hart! Good morning and welcome!' She added teasingly, 'I hear you actually started work yesterday afternoon!'

Chris groaned. 'They told me the whole town would know about it today!'

Rose laughed. 'It'll probably mean you'll get the lion's share of Dr Gilmore's patients today. Everyone will be curious about you. Adrian's coming in today, though, so he can have all his patients back, which will ease the load.' She went on, 'Paul and Graham will be glad to have you here. They've been pressured since the last locum left. Of course we all expected Adrian would come back once he knew about his father.'

'Yes, it would be hard to enjoy yourself, or concentrate on seminars, with that kind of anxiety hanging over you,' Chris agreed as she joined Rose in the office.

'I'll show you your consulting room in a jiffy,' Rose said, reaching for the telephone as a red light began flashing on the switchboard.

While Rose was on the telephone, the other two nurses, Jill Fielding and Carole Summers, arrived. Jill, a farmer's wife, was thirtyish, Carole was in her early twenties and vivaciously pretty and bouncy. Both nurses welcomed Chris warmly and quizzed her about the hit-and-run accident. Chris began to feel as though she had achieved unwarranted notoriety.

Rose came off the phone and took Chris to the room she would be using and pointed out where everything was. Swooping round, she checked that the examination couch was properly prepared with clean sheet, cover blanket, paper headrest, and the steps were handy. Then she laid out the sphygmomanometer on the polished pine desk, opened a box of tissues and placed a sterile pack of rubber gloves near the stainless steel sink.

'You've brought your own stethoscope, I suppose?' she queried, and Chris nodded.

Rose pulled out a drawer and said, 'You'll find all the gynae examination instruments in here.' She looked around thoughtfully. 'I think that's everything.'

It was a thoroughly modern surgery, and Chris looked around and thought enviously how different it was from the clinic in Mali! They had many up-to-date medical aids there, but not in such congenial surroundings. She doubted that this surgery ever ran out of anything.

Rose said, 'If there's anything you need, just ask.' She paused at the door. 'I won't send any patients in until you've had a few minutes to familiarise yourself. I'll bring you the record cards in a minute. You might like to browse.'

'Thanks,' Chris said. Knowing a little of a patient's medical history was always helpful, especially when you were a stranger to them. It helped to allay nervousness and induce confidence if the locum had bothered to find out a few facts about the patient beforehand.

She was perched on the edge of the desk reading a medical card when her door opened and a smiling face appeared round it. 'Hi!' A tall, lean man with thinning sandy hair came in. 'Ready for kick-off?'

Chris grinned. 'Just about!' Her visitor was Dr Graham Winslowe. She had met him and the other doctor in the practice, Paul Czernick, on her first visit to Mount William.

Graham plonked a small brown paper-wrapped package on her desk. 'From Jen—orange marmalade. I didn't want to forget to give it to you. And she said to tell you the lad you rescued on Saturday is doing fine. No complications.'

Graham's wife, Jennifer, was Director of Nursing at the Central Highlands Hospital, Chris remembered.

'I'm glad to hear that,' she said with relief. 'He's lucky.'

'Lucky you were on the spot,' said Graham. He glanced

around the room. 'Just yell if you need help, and don't be afraid to ask for a second opinion!'

Chris grinned. 'Thanks! And thank your wife for the marmalade. It's the one thing I don't seem to have in my cupboard.'

'You must come to dinner with us one evening soon,' Graham said before he vanished, leaving Chris feeling touched by the friendliness of her colleagues. If only she could quell the strong feelings she still had for Adrian . . .

Rose interrupted her momentary reverie by putting her head round the door to say, in her soft Scottish burr, 'If you're ready, I'll send the first victim in. There are three waiting for you.' She added with a mischievous smile, 'You've got Mrs Pickles this morning!'

Chris's eyebrows rose. 'Oh? Is she special?' she asked cautiously.

'*She* thinks she is!' said Rose. 'Mrs Pickles is the biggest hypochondriac in the Central Highlands. She loves a new doctor! But you can have Mrs Wardrop first.'

Chris groaned. 'Thanks for the warning.'

She moved behind the desk and glanced again at Mrs Wardrop's medical card as she waited a little nervously for her first patient to enter. At a hesitant tap on the door she called out, 'Come in!'

A red-haired, very obviously pregnant woman entered the room and smiled diffidently. 'Good morning, Doctor,' she greeted Chris in a quiet voice as she sank heavily into the patient's chair.

For one vivid moment, Chris was back in Mali and the face before her was gaunt black, not healthy white. She blinked and pulled herself together.

'Good morning, Mrs Wardrop,' she said, smiling. 'I expect Sister told you that I'm Dr Hart, standing in for Dr Gilmore.' The woman nodded. Chris went on, 'You've come for your monthly check-up, is that right?'

'Yes . . .' Suddenly, Mrs Wardrop blurted out, 'I've never been to a woman doctor before!' Then she looked painfully embarrassed and blushed scarlet.

Chris flinched. It was incredible that some people could

still regard women doctors as a novelty and, as she was sure this young woman's tone indicated, feel uncertain of their capabilities simply because of their sex.

She said briskly, 'Well, let's see what your blood pressure's like first.' She reached for the sphygmomanometer and walked around the desk to her patient, asking a few pertinent questions as she fastened the rubber cuff around her arm and began to pump it up.

A few minutes later, as Mrs Wardrop was dressing and Chris was writing on her record card, she said, 'Well, everything seems to be fine, Mrs Wardrop. I don't think that slight swelling of your ankles is anything to worry about, but let me know if it gets worse. Don't hesitate to come in before the next appointment if you feel anything unusual is happening, will you?' She added with a smile, 'What are you hoping for, a girl or a boy?'

'I'd like a boy,' the young woman replied, 'but Eric, my husband, wants a girl. I almost wish it was twins.'

Chris laughed sympathetically. 'Well, I'm afraid not—not this time!'

Mrs Wardrop picked up her handbag. 'Thank you, Doctor.' She paused at the door and seemed more assured now. 'I hope you'll like it in Mount William, Dr Hart.'

Chris heaved a small sigh of gratification as her first patient departed. The woman's nervousness had quickly disappeared and she had chatted unselfconsciously after the first few minutes. She hoped the rest of her patients would be as amenable.

A minute or two after Mrs Wardrop had gone, Chris's second patient came in. Already she was feeling more at ease, but she had made one change. She had shifted the patient's chair to one side of the desk. Dealing with people across a barrier had never appealed to her. Some said it established authority, but Chris disagreed. She wanted patients' confidence, not their awe.

The morning passed swiftly. By coffee-break time, Chris had seen half a dozen patients and was really into the swing of it. Rose looked in after one patient had left and said, 'If you want to snatch a few minutes at the coffee urn, now's your chance. You're up to schedule.' She added kindly, 'Everything OK?'

'I hope so!' Chris followed her out and Rose showed her to the kitchen-cum-lounge. Chris went over to the coffee machine. It was all so civilised, she thought, like the hospital. And she couldn't help seeing the Mali clinic in her mind's eye, comparing and envying all this on Mali's behalf.

'Good morning, Chris.'

She turned and found Adrian smiling at her. Idiotically her heart began to pound. 'Oh, hello, Adrian—you did finally wake up then?'

He looked contrite. 'I humbly apologise for being so unsociable yesterday! I went down as though I'd been felled with a sledgehammer.'

'No need to apologise. I had a very pleasant lunch with your parents. We didn't really miss you!'

She felt she was being flip, but he made her feel brittle. He looked different this morning. The tiredness had almost gone from his eyes, the drawn look from his skin. His hair was neatly slicked back and he was wearing a well-cut sports jacket, grey flannel trousers and a collar and tie. It was no use denying that he made her heart beat faster. It was a fact of life and it was better to be able to cope with it. Her reaction to him surprised her, that was all. She hadn't thought feelings that had lain dormant for so long could be resurrected so spontaneously.

'No, I dare say you didn't,' he replied drily, and then, 'How's it going this morning? No difficult patients?' He strolled to the urn and filled a cup with black coffee, then stood looking at her, cradling the cup in his hands until she was sure it must be burning his palms.

It was, but it was a small torture he was inflicting on himself in an effort to lessen the greater torture of looking at Chris. He still couldn't quite believe she was there, in his own practice, seeing his father's patients, back in his life . . . Only she wasn't back in his life, not in the sense he'd always wanted her to be. And it wasn't likely she ever would be. She'd been quite definite eight years ago. Chris wasn't a woman who lightly changed her mind. And he wasn't a man who lightly changed his. It had taken him only half a day to realise that, despite the years, despite the belief he had forgotten her, he still loved her. It was a painful realisation. He wished she hadn't come to Mount William. Or that he hadn't come home. On the other hand . . . cautiously he considered the remote possibility that a benevolent Fate had brought them together after all this time, on purpose.

Adrian looked into the sensitive grey eyes and wished he could read her mind. All he could see was something that told him she had suffered, that life had left some scars. He suspected there was personal grief, but also knew she would have suffered for the people she was trying to help in Mali. Compassion had always been a strong trait in Chris. She was, he had no doubt, a very good doctor.

'I've enjoyed it,' she said, answering his question. 'Three pregnant mums, two bad backs requiring certificates to be off work, a referral to an eye specialist and one hypochondriac. That's variety!'

'You got Mrs Pickles?' he guessed, laughing. 'You didn't deserve her on your first morning!'

'Rose did warn me.'

'What was her trouble this time?'

'Gallstones. Her diagnosis.'

'What did you say to her?'

Chris smirked. 'I told her she probably had a rare form of the disease since her symptoms weren't typical, and that we wouldn't be able to make a definite diagnosis until she lost some weight. I gave her a diet sheet and some exercises and a prescription for indigestion powder. She seemed delighted. She told me proudly that she's a real puzzle to the doctors.'

Adrian burst out laughing again. 'If you're around long enough, Chris, I can see you'll cure her!'

Chris glanced at the clock on the wall as, in the silence that suddenly developed, she heard its loud electric click. 'I'd better be getting back.'

She tilted her head in that innocently alluring way she still had and looked at him through lowered lashes which were as long and silky as ever. Adrian struggled with a desire to reach out, tip her small rounded chin up and kiss the rosy lips that were so inviting, but he was afraid of alienating her.

'See you later,' he said.

When Chris returned to the lounge at lunchtime, only Paul Czernik was there. She had met the young doctor only very briefly before. He rose politely as she entered, his dark eyes taking in every inch of her and approving of what he saw.

'Dr Hart—good afternoon,' he greeted her in a measured tone. Although born in Australia, he had a slight European accent, acquired no doubt from his parents. He added, 'I hope I may call you Chris?'

'Of course! And may I call you Paul?'

He held out his hand. 'I'm glad you decided to join us, Chris. Did you have a good morning?'

'It went smoothly, I think. I enjoyed it.'

'I'm sure the patients did too,' he said gallantly, devouring her with his melting brown eyes, and accompanying his words with a smile that was mildly flirtatious. He was very good-looking, she thought, deeply tanned, with dark blond hair and an athletic physique.

'I think one or two would still prefer the more solid and reliable Dr Gilmore,' she commented. 'Women doctors are not too common around here?'

'There have been several at the hospital. We've not had one in this practice before, though. Of course we are still a rather conservative community, I suppose. Country people sometimes are. But they'll get used to you. Your prompt action yesterday will have earned you an instant good reputation.'

Chris felt more and more embarrassed about the incident now. She had done very little, there being little she could do in the circumstances. It was just lucky she had seen the accident and the boy had not lain undiscovered long enough to suffer from exposure and untreated shock.

'I understand you hope to return to Africa in a few months,' Paul Czernik said.

Chris nodded. And for the next few minutes she found herself talking about the clinic in Mali. Paul's questions suggested genuine interest on his part. Adrian came in as they were talking and hovered, interposing a question now and then, until Chris stopped abruptly, feeling that she was talking too much.

'Sorry. I must be boring you rigid!'

'Not at all,' Paul assured her. His eyes drifted over her, indicating that his interest was not entirely for what she had been saying. 'It's fascinating, I admire your tenacity. It must be a depressing job at times.'

'Yes, it can be,' she agreed soberly. 'What you're doing seems no more than a drop in the ocean.' She caught not his eyes, but Adrian's, and lost herself for a moment in their unfathomable brown depths. She went on quickly, as she looked away, 'But some positive steps are being made. I wish they'd show more of the progress on television instead of only the misery. People aren't just looking for handouts, they're making positive efforts to help themselves, and succeeding. Things are slowly improving.'

Paul stood up to go and Chris, noticing the time, was about to follow when Adrian detained her with a suggestion.

'I'm going over to the hospital when I've finished here this afternoon. To see young John Portman. Would you care to come?'

Chris was surprised and pleased at his offer. 'Yes, I would.'

'I'm sure he'd like to thank his rescuer.'

'Oh, I don't want any fuss,' Chris said doubtfully.

He shook his head. 'Of course not. But Jen told Graham that he told the nurses after his leg had been set that he was rescued by a very pretty lady!'

Chris laughed. 'How old did you say he was?'

'Fourteen! We believe in vitamin supplements around here!' he joked, and they laughed together easily.

As the moment of mirth passed, Chris felt a sharp stab to her heart. They'd always laughed together easily, at silly jokes, fatuous remarks, seeing the absurdity of things when no one else could, sharing small private moments with a special kind of rapport because of a kindred sense of humour. It was nice to discover they still could, even fleetingly. But it hurt.

'We'll probably be through here by five-thirty today,' Adrian predicted. 'See you then.'

For Chris the afternoon sped as swiftly as the morning and she found herself faced with as wide a variety of ailments and conditions as earlier. Some of the patients wanted to talk more than others and some showed open curiosity about her. By the end of the session she was a little behind in her appointments. An ulcerated leg had required longer to dress than a standard appointment, and one small child had proved difficult at first mainly because of his mother fussing over him instead of leaving him to Chris's more expert handling. Eventually the hysterics subsided and Chris was able to examine his infected and very painful ear.

It was, therefore, well after five-thirty when she packed the sphygmomanometer back in its box and stowed it in the drawer along with other items from her desk. She retrieved her bag and went to find Adrian, hoping he would have waited and not gone without her.

Rose was still in the office but the other two nurses had gone. So had the other doctors.

'Has Adrian gone too?' Chris asked.

'Not yet. He's still with a patient. His last.' Rose gave Chris a sympathetic look. 'Well, you survived! Tired?'

'I've been tireder! It was an easy day really.'

'True, it wasn't as frantic as some,' Rose agreed. 'We're often here till seven or later, even on days when there's no late surgery. Did I mention that we have surgery until eight on Wednesdays and Fridays?'

'Yes, you did. I'll be rostered, presumably?' asked

Chris.

Rose confirmed that she would be, then said, 'Are you going up to the hospital with Adrian?'

'Yes, to say hello to the lad I brought in yesterday.'

'Good. I expect Jen Winslowe will show you round—or Adrian will if she's not there. Jen's a character. Bubbling over with energy and ideas. She's the best DON they've ever had up there. You'll like her.'

Rose broke off as the swing door which led to the consulting rooms squeaked and a man came up to the reception desk. 'I'll pay my account now, Sister,' he said, attracting Rose's attention. 'Doctor says I don't need another appointment.'

'All right, Mr Patterson,' Rose said, and went out to attend to him.

A moment later Adrian poked his head around the other door into the office. 'Shan't be a minute, Chris.'

'No rush!'

It was almost like old times, she suddenly thought, meeting as they went off duty, sometimes having to wait for each other because punctuality was a virtue that doctors were not often able to indulge.

A few minutes later they left the centre and Chris followed Adrian to the hospital in her own car. The Central Highlands Hospital was on the other side of town and pleasantly situated on a rise with views over farmland and to the mountains.

'We didn't have a hospital here until five years ago,' Adrian told her. 'People had to go to Ararat or Ballarat. But, with the growth in tourism and a bit of light industry moving into the town, the population grew and eventually warranted a hospital. It's not a large one, but there's room for expansion if the town continues to grow as we expect it to do.'

Adrian had a couple of other patients besides John Portman whom he wanted to see, so, when they arrived, he handed Chris over to Jennifer Winslowe, who showed her around and introduced her to practically every member of staff they bumped into and to most of the patients as well.

'I'll take you along to John Portman's room and leave you, if you don't mind,' Jen said eventually. 'I've got a couple of things to do before I pack up for the day.'

Chris said, 'Thank you for taking the time to show me round, Jen. I know how busy you must be.'

Jen looked her over. 'A pleasure,' she said, and it sounded sincere. She grinned. 'You knew Adrian years ago, didn't you?'

Chris nodded. 'We worked together for a while.'

'Well, it must be nice your meeting up again,' said Jen, and Chris's heart sank a little at her meaningful tone. She didn't want Jen Winslowe or anyone else to get the wrong idea about her and Adrian, but what could she say?

'Mrs Winslowe . . .' A nurse came scurrying along the corridor and Jen, having pointed Chris in the direction of John Portman's room, dashed off with the girl on some urgent errand.

Almost at the ward door, Chris met up with Adrian.

'Nice timing!' he said, as they went in together.

A maid was collecting the boy's meal tray. Adrian held the door for her, then marched over to the bed. 'Hello there, John,' he greeted the young patient. 'They've put Humpty together again properly, I hope?' He tapped the plaster cast on the boy's leg.

'So do I, Dr Gilmore!' John said. 'But I reckon the bike's a write-off. Dad went and picked it up. He says it'll only be good for parts.'

'At least you're still good for better than that!' joked Adrian. 'I'm glad to hear you were wearing your helmet. It might have been a different story otherwise.' He ran his eye over the traction, then pulled Chris forward. 'I suppose you remember who this is?'

John Portman grinned. 'Are you the lady who found me?'

Chris nodded, and Adrian said, 'This is Dr Hart,

John. You were lucky she saw the accident. She's very anxious to know how you are. And she got a good look at the idiot who clipped you, so with a bit of luck they'll catch him.'

Chris said, 'Actually I didn't bring you in on my own, John. Fortunately a camper-van came along and helped. The campers brought you to the hospital in their van to save time.'

'Gee, I missed all the fun!' joked John. 'I don't remember much. I must have been out cold.' Gingerly, he rubbed the dressing on his cheek. 'They reckon it won't leave a scar . . .' But he looked anxious.

Adrian reassured him. 'No, that's right. It'll be a bit red for a while, but it'll heal right over and I promise there won't be a scar.'

They stayed for a few minutes longer, chatting to the lad, who asked Chris to sign his plaster cast before she left. As they were leaving, his parents arrived and Chris was obliged to accept their effusive thanks. She was beginning to feel quite unworthy of all the fuss.

When they finally left the hospital it was after seven.

'How about dinner at our place?' asked Adrian as they walked to their cars. 'Mother won't mind, and you can't want to cook for yourself tonight after a hard day.'

Chris shook her head. 'Thanks, but I'd better get used to it! It's kind of you, Adrian, and your mother, but I'm quite happy on my own.'

Yes, he thought, I believe you are. You wouldn't still be single otherwise. I wonder how many other hearts you've broken, and did someone once break yours?

'All right,' he said, 'but remember, Chris, you're always welcome at the Gilmores'. We don't want you running out on us because you're homesick or lonely or feeling neglected.'

Chris grimaced. 'Oh, Adrian, as if I'd run out on you! And if I suffered from homesickness I'd never have got as far as Africa and stayed there for years. But thanks anyway, I do appreciate it.'

She followed him to the car-park and along the road for a short distance until, with a sharp blast on the car horn, he turned left and she, with an answering toot, drove straight on, feeling as they parted irrationally bereft.

But once inside the house, with the lights on and the central heating warming up the rooms, busying herself in the kitchen, Chris relaxed into a comfortable feeling that was almost contentment. She was just about to heat the wok for a stir-fry when the doorbell pealed.

'Adrian!' she exclaimed as she opened it.

He looked a little sheepish. 'Mother sent this!' He held out a foil-covered plate.

'Come in . . .' His sudden appearance made her feel flustered.

He seemed to fill the small hall. 'I know you don't want to be fussed over, Chris, but Mother has a passion for making sure people are well fed and not neglected. I had to bring it.'

'Your mother is very kind. Thank you so much.'

'She reckons you won't get around to making apple pies for yourself,' Adrian said, and then, backing away, 'Well, I'd better let you get on with it . . .' Despite his words he seemed reluctant to go.

Chris was equally reluctant to let him go, yet she had no reason to detain him. 'Well, thank Janet very much,' she said again, 'and assure her I'm about to eat a most nutritious stir-fry concoction from my trusty old wok! I promise you I won't starve.'

'You don't look like someone who overeats,' he pointed out with a critical glance at her slim figure.

Chris shrugged. 'I was always a mini-person,' she said without thinking. It was a word from the past and it hung between them as their eyes met. He had always called her his mini-person. Now the affectionate term sounded hollow. She cursed herself for the slip. It was going to be difficult after all. There was an unbridged gulf between them, yet so many memories to inflict hurt.

Adrian stood for a moment, unable to go as he knew he should, and quickly. Hardly aware of himself, he took a step towards her and recklessly did what he had wanted to do earlier in the day. He tilted her chin with a fingertip and kissed her.

Chris was holding the pie with both hands so she couldn't prevent him, but the dish stopped him drawing her close. He glimpsed the startled look in her widening eyes, but he was sure he wasn't mistaken when the rigidity of her mouth almost perceptibly softened under his lips.

He drew back, alarmed because he might have offended her, that he might have imagined her faint response. 'I suppose I shouldn't have done that,' he said, smiling to make light of it. At least with both hands clutching the pie-dish she couldn't slap his face.

There was a faint trembling at the corners of her mouth, despite the way she had tightened her lips, and a coolness in her eyes and voice that seemed to him just a shade forced when she said, 'No, you shouldn't have, and I hope you won't do it again.'

'There was a time when . . .' he heard himself murmuring daringly.

'That was a long time ago,' Chris said sharply. Her hands were shaking and her heartbeat raced out of control. 'We went our separate ways, Adrian.'

'But our paths have crossed again,' he reminded her. 'Strange, isn't it?'

She shrugged. 'Coincidence. Life is full of them. It isn't significant.'

'Nothing's changed, then?'

'Why should it have?' she countered carefully. Their eyes met, his challenging, hers obstinately refusing to show him how she really felt, how much agony there was in caring.

He thought of her lips, soft under his, the slight yielding of her body to his touch. 'I wonder . . .' he murmured. Was he as sensitive to her mood as he believed, or was it just wishful thinking? He added briskly, 'Goodnight, Chris. Back to your wok, and I hope you enjoy the apple pie!'

# CHAPTER FOUR

ONE DAY was much like any other day in Mount William, but time went quickly for Chris. After three weeks it was hard to believe she had been there so long. She had adapted swiftly to the routines of the medical centre and the social life of the town. Not that she went out and about very much. She preferred to relax at home with books and television. Occasionally Janet Gilmore rang and invited her over for a meal, as did a few other people.

The constant stream of patients who went in and out of Chris's consulting room door presented her with a wide variety of conditions to diagnose and treat, or pass on to others for specialist attention. But none touched her so deeply as Helen Bowden and her small son, who came into the consulting room one morning.

Chris looked at the young mother seated near her and wished she could alleviate the sadness in the woman's eyes, but to offer false hopes would be to make the truth, when it was confirmed, as Chris felt certain it would be, the more cruel. Helen Bowden's arms were clasped tightly around her small son, who sat listlessly on her knees. Chris had examined him thoroughly and carefully questioned his mother.

Now she said, 'I'd like Robbie to have some tests, Mrs Bowden. That will mean going down to Melbourne. I'll talk to the other doctors about it and find out what the usual procedure is.' She paused as the woman's worry lines deepened. 'Perhaps you'd like one of the other doctors here to see Robbie first . . .?'

Mrs Bowden shook her head. 'No, no. I'm sure that isn't necessary.' She moistened her lips and Chris could see she was having difficulty controlling her emotions. 'We can go and stay with my mother. If he has to stay in

hospital . . .' Her voice faded, then she said firmly, 'Is it
. . .?' and then couldn't give voice to her fear.

Chris had realised that Helen Bowden was suspicious
before she'd even come to the surgery. The woman
looked sensible and practical, but not unnaturally she
had probably been trying to pretend that her fears were
groundless for some time. Chris didn't want to insult
her intelligence, but she spoke carefully.

'I can't make a definite diagnosis,' she said. 'That
won't be possible until they've done the blood and
marrow tests.'

'Leukaemia isn't curable, is it?' Mrs Bowden said in a
flat tone, her lips quivering a little.

Chris swallowed hard. She could so easily imagine the
anguish of being told your child had cancer. She said as
encouragingly as she could, 'No, there's no positive
cure, but some forms of leukaemia are very responsive
to treatment, and many patients can expect long
remissions, sometimes for years.'

Robbie's mother turned her face away and looked out
of the window at the square of brilliant blue sky and the
scudding clouds, her face working convulsively as she
struggled with her emotions. After a moment or two she
looked back, and Chris admired the strength that now
showed despite the still anxious eyes.

Helen Bowden smiled bravely. 'He's so young . . .'
she murmured wistfully, then resolutely, 'Well, we'll
just have to see what happens, I suppose.' She hugged
Robbie tightly, resting her chin on his head, and her
eyes were momentarily awash with tears. So were
Chris's.

After a moment, Chris said, 'I'll ask Sister to make
an appointment for you with the specialist as quickly as
possible. Perhaps you could phone—or call in—later on
today?'

Mrs Bowden nodded. She rose and was prising the
small wooden toy her son was still holding, one of the
collection Chris had bought to amuse small patients,
from his reluctant fingers.

Chris said impulsively, 'No—let him keep it.'

Helen Bowden relaxed her grasp. She smiled faintly. 'Thank you, Doctor,' she said quietly. Her control was slipping again and she turned and hurried abruptly out of the consulting room.

Chris gazed after her, feeling deeply depressed. It didn't matter that she would never have children of her own to weep over, she was able to weep over other people's with the same anguish and compassion.

She completed a medical record card for the visit and put it on one side. Later she would consult Adrian about the next step. Then she sat back and worried whether she should have tried to cheer his mother more. She was still worrying when the next patient tapped at the door and came in, grinning broadly.

Oh, no, here comes the comic relief! thought Chris, with an inward groan, as she recognised the type.

'Mr Partridge?' she said briskly, switching on a smile that was not too encouraging for the middle-aged, scruffily dressed man with a day's growth of beard and a stomach that along with his pungent breath was blatant evidence of his liking for alcohol.

He winked broadly. 'That's right, m'dear. Mike Partridge—a bit of a rare bird around these parts! Ha! Ha!' His look was almost a leer and Chris wished she'd left the patient's chair on the far side of the desk. He managed to drag it closer as he lowered his bulk into it.

'What can I do for you?' she enquired pleasantly, and instantly realised that her choice of words was a gift to a character like him.

Mr Partridge clearly fancied himself as a ladies' man and he told her so in oblique terms.

'I meant for your health,' Chris broke in frostily, but that was a mistake too.

He sprawled in the chair and winked lewdly, delivered further innuendoes which he apparently thought very witty and laughed loudly at himself.

Chris gritted her teeth. 'Mr Partridge, there are a lot of patients waiting to be attended to. What's your problem?' She turned on her best unamused expression.

He eyed her uncertainly for a moment, then laughed a little self-consciously. 'Aw, Doctor, I was only trying to make you blush! But now I can see you're one of those tough feminist types. Well . . .' He took a deep wheezing breath. 'It's me heart, see. I get terrible palpitations . . . can't get me breath sometimes . . .' He couldn't resist, however, adding facetiously, 'Of course it might just be the new barmaid down at the pub—she's got these enormous . . .'

'Roll up your sleeve, Mr Partridge,' Chris interrupted, and without her customary gentleness fastened the cuff around the plump hairy arm and pumped it up, keeping her eyes well averted from his face.

She said curtly, 'The best cure for you, Mr Partridge, is not to go to the pub so often. Then you won't suffer from the barmaid or the booze. And you also need to lose a lot of weight,' she finished severely.

She removed the cuff. 'Your heart won't last you as long as it should if you keep on abusing it. You've had some warning signs. Take heed of them.' She sat down again and pulled the prescription pad towards her.

He had listened to her lecture with a smirk on his thick lips, but he made no more fatuous remarks. Chris knew she was wasting her time advising him. Like so many others, Mike Partridge would eventually kill, or nearly kill himself indulging in overeating and getting drunk. She sighed inwardly. And then he'd expect a miracle cure from the medical profession.

Chris did not break for coffee that morning as she was behind schedule. Patients came in a steady stream through the door. She removed stitches from a gashed arm, she wrote prescriptions for an asthmatic, a diabetic and several heart patients. She peered down throats and up noses, examining vaginas and rectums and palpated abdomens and diaphragms. She wrote out referrals and medical certificates and vaccinated overseas travellers. She added to her growing store of knowledge about the inhabitants of Mount William and was gratified by the friendliness of most people. Problem patients like Mr Partridge were rare, and even he had said, 'Cheerio, Doctor, hope you enjoy your stay in Mount William.'

Chris was relieved that settling in had been so easy. She had felt accepted at the Centre from the first day and her colleagues had drawn her into their easy camaraderie as naturally as though they'd always known her. Only Adrian, she thought sometimes, rather wistfully, made her feel uneasy. Because of their past relationship it was impossible to think of him as dispassionately as she did the others.

Rose had asked her home for a meal one evening and she had met Rose's husband, Duncan, an electrician, and their teenage children, who were delighted to tell her:

'We've got a foster-child in Mali!'

They brought our letters and photographs and reports, and Chris was able to give them first-hand details of what life was like in the African country, particularly for those with problems of poverty and health. She was able to answer many of their questions about how organisations like the one through which they sponsored their family operated in the field.

Rose and Duncan seemed to have no regrets about having emigrated from Scotland. They seemed a happy family and Chris envied Rose and Duncan their comfortable relationship and the love they very obviously shared. Duncan had a good job at the hospital, Rose enjoyed her work at the Centre and the children were doing well at school. The future looked bright for them all.

Life did not seem so favourable for the Fieldings, though. Chris suspected that it was only because Rose had done so that Jill invited her home to the farm. At once Chris could see that there was not the same affluence as at the MacLeods' and she suspected that Jill resented it because she kept apologising.

Finally, Chris had rebuked her gently. 'Good

heavens, Jill, you've got a palace here compared to some of the places I've seen!'

Jill had blurted rather sulkily, 'You sound like Royce. He's always telling me to count my blessings.'

Chris regretted her remark. She hadn't meant to sound patronising. Jill obviously suffered from having spent all her life in the same area with little chance to enjoy what she would probably think of as glamour.

'You're lucky,' Jill said, confirming this opinion as they were washing up after the meal. 'You've seen the world. When you're single you can go where you like and do what you like. I envy you.'

'It's all right if you don't mind being a bit lonely sometimes,' said Chris, in a tone that made Jill glance at her sharply.

'I'm surprised you're not married,' she ventured.

Chris should have made a light retort, but with a sudden urge to dispel Jill's festering discontent, and perhaps even to purge herself, she confessed what she had never confessed to anyone before. 'You're very lucky, Jill, having a husband and a family. I can't have children.'

Jill's shock was profound. 'Oh, Chris, how awful . . . but surely . . .'

Chris wanted to end the conversation quickly. 'I haven't yet met a man who didn't want his own children.'

'Plenty of people adopt them.'

'Yes, but most of them don't know they can't conceive before they marry. I do.' She gave a wan smile. 'It's a hard thing to tell a man, on the first date or the hundredth! I just make sure I don't get too involved.' She added anxiously, 'You will treat this as confidential, won't you, Jill? I've never told anyone before, not even my mother!' She smiled wryly at Jill's astonishment. 'I never wanted anyone to feel sorry for me,' she explained.

'I wouldn't dream of telling anyone, Chris,' Jill promised as she let the water out of the sink. She went on soberly, 'I guess I ought to count my blessings more often.' A querying look. 'Is there no hope. I mean, modern technology . . .'

Chris shook her head. 'Modern technology can't put back what was lost. I had what I thought was appendicitis. It turned out to be salpingitis and I had to have surgery. It was just before my finals!'

'It must have been shattering.'

'Yes, it was, but how shattering I didn't realise until I met someone I wanted to marry. It was painful breaking off that relationship so I've avoided serious romances since.' She forced a laugh. 'It's not really as bad as it sounds, Jill. I lead a very full and satisfying life, believe me. If I'd married I probably would never had gone to Mali. There are compensations. Now, can we talk about something else?'

They did, but Chris's thoughts remained with Adrian and she could have kicked herself for blurting out everything to Jill. She couldn't imagine what had come over her. But if it caused Jill to adopt a new perspective on her own life, then it had achieved something. Chris just hoped she would not be tempted to reveal, what she knew to anyone else.

And particularly not to Adrian. She had not seen a great deal of him since the first couple of days in Mount William. He no doubt regretted that small step out of line when he had kissed her. For her it was a moment that too often invaded her thoughts. Was he still attracted to her? she sometimes wondered. She told herself firmly that she did not want Adrian to be interested in her. And yet . . . her own feelings were not dead. She was only too uncomfortably aware of that.

Chris had been invited to the Gilmores' several times for meals, but she had never been alone with Adrian, except briefly once or twice at the Centre, when she had consulted him about a patient. He had been very sympathetic and helpful over young Robbie Bowden and had shared her concern. There had been a moment after they had been discussing it, when he had suddenly

tilted her chin and for an instant she had half expected
him to kiss her, but instead he had said softly,

'You always were vulnerable, Chris.'

The most unexpected happening during her first three
weeks was that Paul Czernik asked her out. Chris had
sometimes been aware that he was sizing her up in the
way a man did who was interested in a woman, but they
only occasionally had a conversation, and she had not
regarded his interest as significant.

It was a little ironic, therefore, that he should
approach her on the very day that Carole Summers had
jokingly warned her about him.

'I think Paul fancies you, Chris,' the young nurse had
said, alarming Chris as well as surprising her.

'I thought he fancied *you*!' Chris replied. Carole
openly flirted with the doctor and when chided by Rose
because he was much older than her, she had said,

'Obviously you don't read modern romances. All the
dishiest heroes are thirtyish!'

Now Carole grimaced. 'No such luck! He prefers
mature women! He doesn't mind pinching my bottom
for a tease and giving me a quick hug and a kiss in the
Treatment Room, but that's only his ego!' She raised
her finely plucked eyebrows which were emphasised
with lurid pink eyeshadow and pouted. 'He hasn't even
made a real pass at me!' She gave Chris a slyly
speculative look. 'But I think he's very sexy, don't
you?'

'You must be talking about me!'

Both girls turned round guiltily at the sound of
Adrian's amused voice. He was leaning languidly in the
doorway, grinning at them.

'Oh—Dr Gilmore . . .' stammered Carole, blushing,
and then regaining her composure, 'Well, actually we
were talking about Paul, but of course you are too, I
suppose—to an older person that is!' She winked at
Chris and stupidly Chris suddenly felt confused as she
met Adrian's dark gaze.

He was trying to look stern. 'Is gossiping about how

sexy men are all you two have got to do?'

Carole replied airily, 'As a matter of fact, I was just explaining to Chris the ins and outs of Medicare and bulk-buying and all that red-tape.'

Adrian commented drily, 'I hope she's now wiser than I am!' And walking out with Chris a moment or two later, he remarked rather archly, she thought, 'Do you think Paul Czernik is rather sexy?'

Taken aback, Chris just raised her face and stared at him. His gaze was inscrutable. 'No more so than any other man I know!' she said lightly, and gave a shaky laugh. Then, pretending indignation, added, 'Not that it's any of your business!'

He dropped a hand briefly on her shoulder. 'No, I suppose it isn't,' he said in a flat tone, and left her.

It was later the same day when Chris had finished seeing her patients and was almost ready to leave that Paul sauntered into her room.

'Finished?'

'Yes, and you?'

'Just,' he said. 'I've got a bit of paperwork to clear up, but that won't take more than a few minutes. I wondered if you'd care to go somewhere for a drink and a meal? I was thinking of a pleasant little restaurant in an old farmhouse just out of town. It's not usually too crowded mid-week.' He gave her a quirky smile. 'They do vegetarian.'

Chris's vegetarianism had caused a few comments at the start, but rather to her surprise, since she had often encountered hostility, sometimes ridicule, there had been considerable interest in her opposition to cruelly to animals and more sympathy than she had expected.

She had kept a low profile because, in a largely farming community, livelihoods depended to some extent, if not entirely, on animals, and farmers were loath to admit that cruelty existed in their methods. In the Centre they had sympathised with her view that it wasn't necessary to kill in order to survive and had been interested, if a bit bemused, by the notion that obtaining protein from animals rather than direct from the food fed to animals was wasteful.

Chris had avoided the heated argument that so often erupted out of prejudice and ignorance, but she had found herself the centre of a lively discussion once or twice. Although Chris didn't expect to turn anyone into a vegetarian overnight, she was gratified to notice that lunches at the Centre suddenly developed a distinct tendency to be meatless. Everyone, it seemed, was, when they stopped to think about it, in agreement about the cruelty of factory farming, but it had never occurred to them to oppose it, even passively, by refusing to buy the products.

Perhaps the most surprising comment had come from Jill, the farmer's wife, who had said thoughtfully on one occasion, 'Well, we keep pigs, but I think we treat them as well as our dogs and cats—they're more or less free-range—but of course they are sent to market in the end, to be killed. I suppose it *is* a kind of betrayal . . .'

When Paul invited her to have a meal out with him, Chris hesitated for a moment or two, not because of any differing views they might have, but because she always hesitated about becoming involved with a man, even casually.

'You must be sick of cooking for yourself all the time,' he urged.

Chris laughed. 'I am! Thank you, Paul. You must have known it was my night for bread and margarine!'

Paul called for Chris at seven-thirty. She was ready, dressed in a warm blue woollen dress with long fitted sleeves as it was a cold night. There was even a touch of frost in the air, despite the fact that it was spring. Chris wrinkled her nose as they went out to the car.

'I thought winter was over!'

'We always get a cold snap just when you're about to mothball your winter woollies,' laughed Paul. 'But it might knock off the 'flu viruses if we're lucky!'

They'd had a minor epidemic of 'flu in the town and

the surgery had been full of patients requiring antibiotics, and there had been one or two calls out to old people who had developed pneumonia and had to be removed to hospital.

Paul took Chris first to the lounge of one of the town's new hotels, and she felt a few eyes noting their entrance with interest and speculation. The trouble with a small town, she thought, was that everyone was the subject of gossip, and no one more than a local doctor. But what did it matter? Paul must be used to it. He wouldn't have brought her to such a public place if he'd minded tongues wagging.

Over a drink, Paul told Chris a little about himself, how his parents had emigrated from Europe in the nineteen-fifties. They were both teachers in Melbourne, he told her, and he had several brothers and sisters. He was the only doctor among them.

'Don't you find life a bit dull up here?' Chris asked. 'I mean, there isn't a lot of social life, is there?'

He shrugged. 'It's not far to Melbourne if you want to go to a show. I go down quite often. But I like it here. I belong to a couple of sporting clubs. I go bushwalking and windsurfing.'

'Windsurfing? Where?' Chris asked eagerly.

'Lake Fyans. It's not far from here,' he told her, and promised, 'When the weather's warmer, I'll take you. Have you done it before?'

She shook her head. 'No, but I'd love to try!' she said, her eyes alight. Ever since she'd first seen windsurfers she'd felt the urge to tackle the sport. It looked so exhilarating.

He squeezed her arm. 'You'll need a bit more muscle than this!'

She pretended to be indignant. 'I'm stronger than you think! Just because I haven't got bulging biceps . . .'

He slid his eyes over her shapely figure. 'But you have other more attractive curves!'

'And I pack a hefty punch,' she joked, but with a warning in her grey eyes.

'You mean you use violence to keep a man at bay?'
There was a challenging twinkle in his eyes.

Chris laughed. 'Self-defence isn't violence!'

'Is that a warning?' Paul's eyebrows lifted slightly.

'Only if you need one!' she parried flippantly.

He drained his glass and slid a hand on to her knee.
'Drink up. It's time we moved or someone else will grab
our table.'

The restaurant in the converted farmhouse was a
roomy, cosy place, and there was a huge log fire burning
in an enormous grate. Two large rooms, probably the
original living and dining-rooms, had been knocked into
one and there was already quite a crowd there, testifying
to its popularity.

'They use all home-grown produce,' Paul told Chris
as they were shown to their table. 'And the meat, eggs
and dairy produce is all free-range, you'll be pleased to
hear.'

Chris murmured, 'Good.' It did not, however, tempt
her to eat those things. Free-range was less cruel perhaps
than factory-farmed, but for years now she had
preferred not to eat animal products at all.

Rather to her surprise, Paul also selected a vegetarian
dish, of which there were several on the menu. The
waitress was pouring the chilled white wine Paul had
brought—it was a BYO, bring-your-own-liquor,
restaurant—into long-stemmed glasses when a couple of
new arrivals caught Chris's eye as she happened to be
facing the entrance. She caught her breath, and Paul
glanced around.

'Well, look who's here,' he murmured.

'They haven't seen us,' Chris said, as Adrian and
Deborah Leigh were ushered to a table on the other side
of the room.

'Probably wouldn't want to,' said Paul. 'They're
pretty thick, those two. Unfortunately, Mount William
doesn't offer all that many good restaurants. I'm afraid
you always see someone you know in a place like this.'
He gave her a quirky smile. 'Your reputation will be set

in concrete by tomorrow!'

'Oh? Are you some sort of local Don Juan?' laughed Chris.

Paul shrugged. 'Mothers with beautiful daughters sometimes appear to think so!'

Her plate of attractively arranged vegetables, rice and tofu in mushroom sauce arrived and Chris dragged her eyes from the couple on the far side of the room. Adrian seemed unaware of them, but in that last second Chris was sure Deborah had glanced their way. It annoyed her that seeing them together had sparked off a pang of jealousy she'd never expected to feel. Chris was angry with herself over such a foolish lapse.

Some time later Adrian must have spotted them or Deborah had told him they were there, for the waitress came over to them and said, 'Dr Czernik, Dr Gilmore would like you and Dr Hart to join them for coffee. I can easily fit in another couple of chairs.'

'Yes, all right . . .' Paul turned and waved an acknowledgement to Adrian.

Chris thought Deborah looked displeased at the intrusion. She wasn't all that keen on joining them herself. Deborah set her teeth on edge and she hated having to admit the reason why. It was sour grapes if anything was, she thought ruefully. She had given up Adrian long ago, so why should she be jealous of anyone he took out? She didn't want him . . . Don't be stupid, she told herself silently, of course you want him. But you can't have him . . .

'Well, you don't let the grass grow under your feet, do you, Paul,' said Deborah, pinning on a smile for the doctor but offering Chris no more than a passing glance.

Paul ignored the remark and made some casual comment of his own, while Adrian looked Chris over with an intense appraisal that slightly unnerved her. Did he disapprove of her going out with Paul because of the young doctor's somewhat racy reputation? She smiled at herself. How like Adrian it was to be protective even when it wasn't needed.

There was an awkward moment of silece between the four of them and Chris wondered what had caused it. Deborah spoke first.

'Have you been notching up any more brave deeds?' she asked Chris flippantly, her laughter high and brittle.

'GPs don't get much chance to do brave deeds,' Chris answered, resenting the other girl's patronising tone. 'We're too busy.'

Deborah's nostrils flared slightly and she fluttered her eyelashes at Adrian. 'How is John Portman, by the way?'

'He's progressing very well,' said Adrian, adding, 'The police caught the hit-and-run driver.'

'Really? How very astute,' said Deborah. 'How do they know he's the one?'

Although Deborah was addressing her remarks to Adrian, Chris answered. 'I saw him clearly when he passed me and I was able to pick him out easily at an identification parade in Ballarat.' It had been an unpleasant experience attending that identification parade, and the killing look the youth she had recognised had given her still haunted her.

'He wasn't from Mount William,' Adrian said.

'What happens now?' Deborah asked. Her gaze was still fixed on Adrian's face as though it was nothing to do with Chris.

Adrian deferred to Chris with a nod, and she said, 'The youth got bail because John's injuries were not too serious. It'll be several months before his trial.'

'I suppose you'll have to give evidence?' Deborah deigned to glance at Chris and her look showed that she was now bored with the subject.

'I may not be here then,' Chris said. 'I've already made a statement, of course.'

'You'll be back in Africa, I suppose,' said Deborah with a nod. 'What a glamorous life some doctors lead!'

Chris did not bother to disagree. She didn't think Deborah would appreciate a description of just how unglamorous being a doctor in Mali was.

They talked for a while longer, until Paul, finishing his coffee, and without consulting Chris, said, 'Well, folks, I think it's time Chris and I were going—if you'll excuse us?'

'So soon?' Deborah sounded delighted. She warned archly, 'Do be careful, Chris. Paul's one of the untamed!'

Chris felt Adrian's speculative gaze of her again and was glad to escape from his scrutiny. In the car, Paul, with a snort of impatience, said, 'Whatever does Adrian see in that young woman?'

'She's very attractive,' Chris murmured.

He flashed her a quick grin. 'Sure, and she's also a pretty sexy lady, but not as pretty or as sexy as you!'

'Don't jump to conclusions,' Chris said quickly.

Paul chuckled. 'Deb would like Adrian for keeps, I dare say.'

'Have they known each other long?' Chris couldn't help her curiosity.

'All their lives, almost, so I gather. She comes from one of the old established Western District grazing families. She and Adrian were at uni together, then she went abroad for several years and when she came back and set up business in Mount William she found he was back here too. I leave it to you to take it from there.'

So Deborah was an even older friend than she was, Chris thought. She wondered if there had ever been an emotional relationship between her and Adrian, when they were at university together perhaps. She could not recall his every mentioning her.

'Do you think they'll marry?' Chris asked casually.

'Probably. Personally I think he'd be better suited to someone like Rita.'

'You mean Rita Vanderhoek?' Chris was surprised at the suggestion. It had never occurred to her to match Adrian with the district nurse whom she had met several times. But Rita was a pleasant, forthright young woman and a very efficient and dedicated nursing Sister. She wasn't a glamour-girl like Deborah Leigh. She had a neat, scrubbed look with a high cheek colour and vivid blue eyes. Her ash-blonde hair was usually coiled into a severe chignon and she was a tall, sturdy-looking girl, serious, but very likeable.

'Still waters run deep,' Paul remarked. 'Rita would be a professional asset as well as brilliant at bringing up kids!'

'Why don't you marry her yourself?' Chris joked.

'She's head over heels in love with Adrian, that's why,' said Paul.

'It's a wonder he isn't married,' Chris said carefully. There must have been plenty of women in his life in recent years, she was thinking.

Paul negotiated a right turn at the town centre and turned down a street leading towards Chris's place. 'Adrian's a very private sort of person. I've a hunch he was let down rather badly once and he isn't keen to put himself in the way of that kind of experience again.'

'Maybe that's it . . .' Chris asked herself, was it possible that she was to blame? Surely not. It was so long ago. Adrian could have had his heart broken a dozen times since then.

Paul braked outside her house. He switched off the engine and turned to her. 'We must do this again some time.'

'Yes—thanks, Paul. It was a lovely evening,' Chris said.

His eyes were admiring. 'How about a sightseeing trip at the weekend? You said you've never explored the Grampians.'

Why not? she thought. 'I'd love to,' she said. 'Thanks.'

He leaned across and as though her acceptance of his invitation constituted one from her, planted a swift, mildly passionate kiss on her mouth in a testing sort of way. When he found no response, he released her. 'I'll see you to the door,' he said, and got out before she could protest.

He did not try to kiss her again. Paul was too smooth an operator, she thought later, to rush things. He said, 'Goodnight, Chris. See you tomorrow.'

'Night, Paul.'

Chris closed the front door behind her and leaned on it for a moment as she listened to his car driving away. She folded her arms and hugged herself briefly. Her thoughts winged away, not with Paul, but to Adrian, and images of Deborah in his arms were an unwelcome invasion.

She went quickly into the bedroom and undressed, wanting the solace of sleep, yet knowing that there were too many thoughts churning around in her head for her to sleep that night.

# CHAPTER FIVE

CHRIS spent the following morning at the hospital, seeing patients who had been admitted recently or were ready to go home. They included a couple of mothers taking new babies home. She had attended both births, and as the first of the babies she had delivered had pushed its way into the world, she had almost started in surprise. Not since she had worked in the obstetrics department of a large London hospital before she went to Africa had she delivered a white baby.

All babies are beautiful, she thought, but it's a pity they don't all have the same chances. As she had handed the healthy baby boy to the nurse she couldn't help reflecting that in Mali, as in many other African countries, the average infant mortality rate was nearly a hundred and fifty per thousand births. And those that survived had a life expectancy of little more than fifty years.

Nearly three-quarters of pregnant mothers and half of newborn babies were anaemic, all newborn babies were underweight and many suffered blindness through Vitamin A deficiency.

'But it's changing slowly,' Chris told Jennifer Graham, the DON, as they were chatting over a cup of tea in Jen's office. 'Ignorance is one of our greatest obstacles, and malnutrition affects just about everybody.'

'It must be difficult to overcome traditional taboos and customs where they interfere with benefit programmes,' Jen sympathised.

Chris nodded. 'There are endless problems in that area. Education is a very slow process. Most Mali women don't of course have babies in hospitals. The midwife comes to the house in most communities. Most of the population live in small villages. Where I am we serve a wide area from a central point where we've built a small unit consisting of an operating room, a small ward, a dispensary and—well, that's about it. We're doing a lot in the training of rural health workers and establishing pharmacies in the villages so people can get the medicines they need more easily.'

'It takes a lot of courage and endurance to tackle problems on that scale,' Jen said.

'Not really. You just do what you see needs to be done as well as you can and try to keep an optimistic eye on the future.' Chris added, 'One of the most rewarding things we do are the vaccination programmes. There was a big measles programme going on when I left. That will save thousands of children's lives. Measles is one of the big child killers in the Third World.'

Presently, as Chris was about to leave, Adrian arrived. He seemed surprised to see her there. 'I didn't notice your car in the car-park.'

'I decided to walk up. I thought I'd better use my legs before they atrophy!'

'Well, if you want to change your mind and wait a couple of minutes, I'll give you a lift back—you are going back to the Centre?'

'Yes. I've got appointments this afternoon.'

'I won't be long,' Adrian said. 'I've just got to sign a discharge for John Portman, your hit-and-run victim. He's going out today. Why don't you come and say hello, or rather, goodbye.'

Chris accompanied him to Men's Surgical and they chatted to John for a few minutes before his parents arrived. John was eager to show off how competent he was on crutches. Chris and Adrian saw them off, then walked across the car-park to Adrian's car. As they were leaving the hospital grounds, she said, 'Would you mind stopping somewhere I can buy a sandwich? I didn't have time to cut one this morning.'

He thought for a moment, then said, 'I'll do better than that, I'll take you out to lunch.'

'No, please,' she protested, 'a sandwich will do.'

He glanced at her. 'All right—but we'll eat it at the

health food store on Aberdeen Street. Have you been there?'

'No, I don't think so. I haven't been around the town much. I seem to be able to get everything I need at the supermarket at my end of town.'

'Mrs Morrissey is a vegetarian. She bakes her own bread and she makes several different hot and cold dishes every day. You might fancy something a bit more substantial than a sandwich. I thought someone would have told you about her.'

'I think Carole mentioned her. It was probably during my first couple of days when I had so much to try and remember.'

As Adrian had promised, the shop sold excellent food, and Mrs Morrissey was delighted to meet Chris.

'I've heard all about you,' she informed her. 'There's not much you can do in this town that no one knows about!'

Chris and Adrian settled themselves on a couple of stools at one end of the counter, and suddenly it was just like the old days, relaxed and companionable.

'You seem to be settling in very well,' Adrian remarked. 'Happy with your accommodation?'

'Yes, it's great. I feel lucky to have rented such a nice house.'

'I haven't forgotten I promised to show you my place some time,' he said. 'But I haven't been out there lately, I've been so busy.'

With Deborah? Chris thought involuntarily, and was annoyed with herself. She said, 'Thanks—some time . . .' not sure whether she wanted it to remain a vague invitation or not.

Adrian then surprised her by saying, 'What about this weekend? I ought to be able to make it on Sunday.'

Chris could see no way around confessing that she was going out with Paul, although she probably would not have mentioned it deliberately. 'I'm sorry, I can't, not this Sunday,' she answered regretfully. 'I-I'm going out with Paul.'

'Paul again!' His exclamation was a trifle scornful.

'Why not?' Chris said defensively. 'He's taking me up to Hall's Gap. I've never been there.'

Adrian stirred his coffee without speaking for a moment, then dismissed the subject briefly. 'Some other time maybe.' He gave her an odd look and, swallowing his coffee, said it was time they moved. Chris followed him out, feeling that she had somehow offended him by having a previous engagement. Or was it just that he didn't care much for Paul?

On the way to the Centre Chris asked him about a patient needing a referral to an ENT specialist and for the duration of the short trip he answered her query about this and one or two other medical matters. Neither of them referred to the weekend again.

His manner, however, made Chris feel uneasy. It had almost seemed as though he was jealous. Surely not? It had all been over between them for years. He had two girlfriends, Deborah and Rita, and possibly others she didn't know about. Could it be, though, a kind of nostalgic dog-in-the-manger attitude? She'd been his girl once, and he didn't want her to be anyone else's? Because she'd virtually jilted him? Some men had a very prickly pride.

When her first patient of the afternoon entered the consulting room, Chris was still more than a little preoccupied and she had to make an effort to concentrate her mind on the catalogue of symptoms the middle-aged woman was giving her.

'It's like a kind of nagging indigestion,' Mrs Slater explained. 'Heartburn, my mother used to call it. And especially in bed at night.'

'If you'll just slip your dress off, Mrs Slater,' Chris requested. She pulled the curtain partially around the examination table.

A few minutes later she was saying to the patient, 'I'd like you to have some X-rays. That'll mean a barium meal first so we can see exactly what the problem is.'

'What's a barium meal?' Mrs Slater asked, covering

her nervousness with amusement. 'It doesn't sound very appetising!'

'No, it isn't!' Chris was obliged to agree. 'But it's quite painless. You'll have to fast for six hours beforehand and then you'll be given a drink containing barium sulphate. Swallowing that will be the unpleasant part. Afterwards you'll be X-rayed. Sometimes a barium meal causes temporary constipation, but if you're normally regular this shouldn't be too much of a problem.'

'Will I have to go to hospital?' asked Mrs Slater anxiously.

'Probably only for the day,' Chris told her. 'Then it will depend on what the X-rays show up.'

A shadow crossed the woman's face. 'You mean I might have ulcers or . . .'

Chris said confidently, 'I don't think it's an ulcer, and I doubt very much that you have a tumour. I think what's troubling you is most probably a hiatus hernia.'

Mrs Slater looked surprised. 'What sort of hernia is that?'

'It's where the upper end of the stomach has pushed up through the diaphragm where the oesophagus passes through from the chest to the abdomen. That's what causes those sensations like heartburn after a meal and particularly when you lie down soon afterwards.'

'Will I have to have an operation?'

Chris explained encouragingly, 'Not necessarily. It's a condition that can cause discomfort and sometimes an operation is advisable, but often a small hiatus hernia can be a very little problem indeed providing you eat small, easily digested meals and avoid strenuous exercise or lying down too soon after meals. Sleeping in a semi-sitting-up position can be helpful too.' She had been drawing a small diagram on her pad as she was speaking and now showed it to the patient. Mrs Slater seemed greatly reassured when she left a few minutes later.

'Well, how was your day?' Paul asked cheerfully when they encountered one another at the end of the day. He had come into her room to give her some brochures from one of the big drug companies.

'I went to the hospital this morning,' Chris told him, 'and this afternoon it's been business as usual.' She grimaced. 'A hiatus hernia I'm ninety per cent sure of, but if it turns out to be a duodenal ulcer after all, I'll eat my hat!'

'Since you don't wear hats that's an idle threat! What else?'

Chris chuckled. 'A sprained ankle, a fungal infection, a case of eczema, rheumatics, hay fever and a "something wrong with me waterworks doctor"!'

'Male or female?'

'Female. Elderly. Cystitis. She'll probably need surgery eventually.' She dragged a weary hand across her brow. 'How was your day?'

'Mixture the same as always. One diagnosis I'd rather not have to make—a melanoma.'

'Early or advanced?'

'Early, fortunately. She'll probably be lucky. I wish everyone who suddenly notices an unusual mole or enlargement or darkening of an existing one would check it out as promptly.'

Carole put her head around the door. 'Oh—sorry. I didn't realise you were here, Dr Czernik.' She waved a manilla envelope. 'Those X-rays, Chris—the hospital sent them down. The ones you asked for Mr Dobson's coccyx!' She giggled and threw a cheeky glance at Paul.

Chris took the envelope. 'Thanks, Carole.'

'Well, I'd better be off,' Paul said as Carole went out. He added, 'Don't forget Sunday. The forecast is fine.'

'Of course I won't forget. I'm looking forward to it,' said Chris. But she wondered if she really was. She liked Paul and a day bushwalking and picnicking appealed to her, but somehow . . .

She dismissed her misgivings, picked up her things and closed her door. As she approached the office area she heard voices. Male voices, raised. Chris was startled and a little alarmed. Relationships were excellent at the

Centre. It was rare to hear a cross word, and certainly not a row like this!

She had no need to go into the office, but as she crept past, she could hear plainly that it was Adrian and Paul who were arguing heatedly. Jill came out, almost on tiptoe, and Chris asked anxiously, 'What's going on?'

Jill raised her eyes heavenwards. 'Don't ask me. One minute all was peace and love and the next Adrian was hoeing into Paul over something. Paul seemed to think it was contemptibly trivial and I'm inclined to think Adrian was overreacting. He's been a bit touchy lately, especially with Paul. It's as though something is bugging him. Maybe it's his father's illness still worrying him.'

'Maybe,' Chris said. She added hopefully, 'No doubt it'll blow over.'

They went out together.


On Saturday morning, Chris had no surgery, so she took the opportunity to stroll around the town's shopping centre. After strolling down the main street, she explored the large undercover shopping centre at one end of the town which merged with an attractively landscaped precinct. It was there that she discovered the Craft Annexe, a collection of craft shops on both sides of a narrow alleyway.

Remembering that it was her mother's birthday soon, Chris went in search of a suitable present. She was considering a display of bark paintings when a loud familiar voice grated on her ears.

'So you've deigned to visit us at last!'

Deborah Leigh was bearing down on her, a vision splendid in pink, very form-hugging pants and a purple smock, her blonde hair swept up into a chignon on top of her head. She really was a stunning woman, Chris thought, and was ashamed of the jealousy that suddenly assailed her as she thought of Deborah and Adrian together.

'Is your shop here?' Chris asked.

'It is. Come along and I'll show you.' Deborah caught hold of Chris's arm, but the gesture was not one of warmth, Chris felt, it was just the girl's flamboyant manner.

They walked to the end of the alleyway and Chris spotted the sign DEBORAH'S POTS before her companion pointed it out. Deborah indicated the display window. 'We're getting ready for Christmas. It's a good time for selling my kind of stuff.'

Inside Chris was introduced to Deborah's assistant, Noreen, who was putting price tags on a new consignment of dark brown glazed mugs and plates and other earthenware.

'Do you sell other people's work as well as your own?' Chris queried, glancing round the well stocked shelves.

Deborah nodded. 'Yes. There are several potters working in Mount William and round about. They're producing some very fine work.'

Chris decided that pottery was just what her mother would like. 'I'd like to buy something for my mother,' she said. 'It's her birthday soon.'

'You don't have to feel obliged to,' Deborah said.

'I don't. Mum loves pottery.'

'Well, have a look around,' invited Deborah. 'The displays are mostly arranged under individual potters' names.' She was showing Chris some interesting pieces when the telephone rang and Noreen called her.

For the first couple of minutes Chris could hear only a murmur from the office at the rear of the showroom, but all at once Deborah's voice rose as though she wanted to be overheard.

'. . . our usual haunt, darling? I'll book the table. Of course I don't mind, I know how busy you are. Yes, I want to talk to you about our weekend in Melbourne . . . I'm looking forward to it . . .'

There was more, but in lower tones again. Chris guessed that the caller was Adrian and she wished that this knowledge didn't make her feel resentful. Deborah came back just as Chris had selected a set of fluted ramekins with chunky handles from Deborah's own pottery collection.

'Sorry about that,' said Deborah. 'It was Adrian.'

Just in case I hadn't guessed, thought Chris. 'Oh, was it?' she said offhandedly, handing the ramekins to Deborah. 'My mother will love these. I'd buy masses of these beautiful pieces for myself if I were staying permanently.' She handled a bowl reflectively, and smiled. 'It's very tempting!'

'What? To buy pots or stay in Mount William?' demanded Deborah, a suspicious glint in her eyes.

Chris laughed. 'Both! But I'm afraid I can't do either. I'm going back to Africa after Christmas.'

Deborah regarded her reflectively. 'Don't you ever think you'd like to settle down, or aren't you the marrying kind?'

The tightness around Chris's heart was like a plaster cast. 'I haven't given it much thought,' she lied. 'It just hasn't come up.'

Deborah had been looking for reassurance, apparently, and now smiled with relief as she stuffed the tissue-wrapped ramekins into an art-deco plastic carrier. Nevertheless she seemed compelled to ask, 'Were you and Adrian—er—close—when you knew each other before?'

Chris hoped a rush of colour to her cheeks would not betray her. 'We went around together for a while,' she said casually. And then added, 'Nothing for you to worry about. That's all water under the bridge.'

Deborah seemed a little embarrassed. 'I just wondered, that's all . . .'

Chris felt her irritation with the woman growing. She said a trifle tartly for her, 'If there's any competition around, Deborah, it isn't me!' She glanced at her watch, eager to escape now. 'I must go. I've a few things still to do.'

She walked out of the shop feeling all churned up inside. Which she had no right to feel, she thought with shame. Just because she didn't care for Deborah Leigh's rather patronising manner, there was no reason to feel uptight because Adrian was probably going to marry the girl.

Chris arrived back at her house soon afterwards and had barely unpacked her groceries and put them away when there was a knock at the door. A woman she felt was slightly familiar was on the doorstep. She looked rather frantic.

'I'm so sorry to bother you on a Saturday,' she said, 'but as we're almost neighbours . . .'

'Mrs Fellowes, isn't it?' Chris said, remembering the name at last. A week or so ago she'd found one of the Fellowes children outside her house screaming. He'd fallen off his skate-board and grazed his knee. She'd taken him inside, dressed the knee and meanwhile sent one of the other children to fetch his mother.

The woman nodded. 'I'm afraid it's Jason again.'

'What has he done this time?' Chris asked, with an indulgent smile. Jason, she had gathered, was somewhat accident-prone.

'He's sick,' Mrs Fellowes said. 'I thought it was just the 'flu. He has a temperature and a headache and he was playing up a bit, but it seems to be worse.'

'How much worse?'

'Well, he's had a sort of convulsion and his neck seems to be stiff.'

'Has he had polio vaccination?' Chris asked promptly.

'Oh, yes . . .'

'Is there a rash?'

'No, I don't think so.' Mrs Fellowes added hopefully, 'He says he wants the lady doctor who fixed his knee.' She smiled. 'He quite took to you, Dr Hart.'

Chris knew she could refer Mrs Fellowes to the duty doctor for the weekend, but as it was only a few houses further down the street and she'd treated the child before, she decided to go herself. It was a case for immediate hospitalisation if what she suspected proved to be the case.

As she was about to leave the hospital some time later, Chris saw Adrian and for some reason his unexpected appearance made her face flood with colour. He strode over to the car and spoke to her through the open window.

'Hello!' He sounded surprised to see her. 'What brings you here today? I thought you were off this weekend.'

'I am, but a neighbour was anxious about her little boy. I'd treated him for a graze once before when he fell off his skate-board outside my house, so I went along to see him.'

'Presumably, as you're here, he was a hospital case this time?'

'Yes. Meningitis.'

He nodded gravely. 'How old is the child?'

'Ten.'

He seemed reluctant to break off the conversation, and yet he seemed to have nothing to say to her. Chris felt awkward too and the atmosphere was for a few seconds, highly charged. Then Chris said, 'Well, I'd better be going.'

Adrian removed his hand from the window frame. 'I hope you have a nice day tomorrow.'

'Oh—yes, thanks. The forecast is fine . . .' For a moment her mind had gone blank and she had forgotten her sightseeing trip with Paul. 'I'm not so keen on bushwalking, I want to do it in the rain!'

'I'm sure Paul will find somewhere cosy to shelter if it rains,' Adrian said in a tone edged with scorn.

Surprised, Chris almost retorted that she hoped he'd enjoy his tête-à-tête dinner with Deborah, which was what she was sure they had been arranging when he'd called the shop, but she resisted the temptation. He might think she cared about it. Which she didn't, she told herself firmly.

When Sunday dawned, Chris felt even less sure she

wanted to go bushwalking with Paul, but she could hardly get out of it now. She pulled on jeans and a skivvy under a warm sweater because he'd warned her it might be cold and would certainly be windy if they climbed the Pinnacle. She took a padded windproof jacket as extra insulation.

She had offered to bring the lunch, and as she lugged the basket to the front door, Paul tooted his horn. He looked more casual than she had so far seen him. He was wearing jeans too, and an anorak. As she watched him stow the picnic basket in the boot, Chris caught herself wishing it was Adrian she was going to spend the day with.

Paul said, 'I hope you're feeling fit. We're going to do quite a bit of walking today.'

'Don't worry, I'm a good walker,' Chris assured him. 'I used to go bushwalking with . . .' She caught herself nearly saying, 'with Adrian' just in time and finished, ' . . . with friends when I was younger. And I walk a lot in Mali, if not always for the sheer pleasure of it.'

'Was one of your bushwalking friends Adrian?' Paul asked, putting two and two together more adroitly than she'd expected.

'We were both part of a fitness cult at the time,' Chris said, convincingly, she hoped.

'When you were both at South City General?'

'Yes . . . I was an intern . . .' She broke off, reluctant to become involved in talking about Adrian and the past. She tried to change the subject by commenting on the scenery, but Paul was not to be deflected so easily.

'Were you more than just colleagues?' he asked, taking a bend rather wide and startling a flock of ibis probing for tadpoles in a swampy paddock. Even Chris's delighted exclamation as the birds rose into the air did not deflect him, and as they passed the spot he asked the question again.

'If you must know, yes, for a time,' Chris replied, a shade irritably.

He glanced at her. 'And some fires die down but are

never quite extinguished, eh?'

'What do you mean?'

'There's still something pretty volatile between you two.'

'Rubbish, Paul. It was eight years ago.' She didn't want to lie, but she didn't want an inquisition. 'There's nothing between us now and not likely to be.'

Paul negotiated another bend with rather less recklessness than the previous one. 'Good! I was hoping you'd say that.'

'Does it matter?' Chris said carefully. 'I'll be back in Africa in a few months, don't forget.'

He slid her a meaningful glance. 'I wasn't thinking of anything permanent, Chris. I just wouldn't want to tread on anyone's toes. Adrian's been rather touchy lately—I thought it might have been because I . . . well, showed I liked you.'

Chris was a bit dismayed at the turn the conversation was taking. She said bluntly, 'I hope you're not anticipating an affair, Paul, just because I've gone out with you twice. Because you're reading me wrongly if you are. Let's be clear about that.'

He didn't answer immediately and Chris stared into the deep blue mountain ranges they were approaching with misgiving, wishing she hadn't come. Finally he said rather dryly, 'One of the things I like about you, Chris, is your directness. You don't beat about the bush. The patients like that too, so I've heard.' He turned and smiled, a smile full of charm and persuasion. 'But what's wrong with—a little affair? Surely you sometimes . . .'

'No, I do not!' Chris said vehemently. 'And if going out with you is going to be taken to mean . . . well, we'd better turn round and go back right now.'

'Don't be hasty,' he soothed. 'I'm not going to try and seduce you. But I suspect that there's a very passionate nature lurking under that rather cool, contained exterior you present to the world. There's a lot of emotion that needs an outlet, I'm sure . . .'

Chris coped by being facetious. 'Now you're being clinical!'

'Am I?' He was smiling as he lightly stroked her thigh. Fortunately another bend in the road forced him to put his hand back on the wheel. 'You can be very tantalising, Chris.'

She forced laughter. 'Paul, I think what you need is a good brisk bushwalk and a stiff climb to the top of some mountain. That'll do more for your libido than I will!'

He chuckled. 'Never!'

He did not pursue the subject after that, for which Chris was grateful. 'We'll go to Mackenzie Falls first,' he told her decisively after a few minutes' silence.

Chris nodded. She didn't care where they went. It was all fresh and interesting to her, but she knew she would have enjoyed the beautiful scenery and the rugged wildness of the mountains much more without the threat of Paul maybe any moment making a pass at her. She tried to put the thought from her mind and concentrated on spotting wildflowers in the bush.

The climb down from the road to the magnificent Mackenzie Falls was an easy one and Chris had no trouble keeping up with the athletically fit Paul. At the bottom they stood and gazed for some time at the roaring curtain of water that fell into a dark mysterious pool, sending up clouds of spray in which rainbows flickered and darted like sprites. Great grey rocks crouched like basking amphibians at the edge of the pool and the ferns and creepers provided secret hiding places for rock spirits, Chris thought fancifully, mindful that the area had been populated once by aboriginal tribes.

'This is an enchanted place,' she breathed softly, inhaling the subtle scents of eucalyptus and mint bush and the cool earthiness of the place. There was a magic there, she felt, and unbidden came the desire to share her delight in it not with Paul but with Adrian. She dared not look at Paul in case a glance from her might be misinterpreted.

'Let's explore a bit,' she said, and set off into the bush around the waterfall. Despite the roaring of the water, the babbling of a stream gushing over rocks out of the pool, occasional loud bird calls and the cracking of twigs beneath their feet, it was a tranquil place with an almost sacred atmosphere.

'There are aboriginal caves throughout the Grampians,' Paul told her as presently they sat on a rock near the waterfall. 'About forty rock shelters, most of them with aboriginal paintings on the walls, have been found.' He got up and offered his hand to her. 'Come on. We're going to Zumsteins next.'

'Tell me about it.' Chris pretended not to see his helping hand. She sensed that if she grasped it he would not let go.

'It's a wildlife sanctuary, mainly for kangaroos and wallabies. Also a great picnic spot. I thought we'd have ours there.'

They climbed back up to the road where they'd left the car. Chris was breathless with the exertion, but she felt exhilarated. Paul laughed as she struggled up the last bit.

'Whacked?'

'Of course not! That was just a pacer!' she panted.

'It's steeper and further to the Pinnacle.'

'I'm ready!' she said recklessly.

They did not see many kangaroos at Zumsteins. More would come in later in the day from the bush to be fed, Paul remembered. But they had lunch in pleasant surroundings and then set off again, this time to climb up to the Pinnacle.

As Paul had warned, it was a long climb to the top, and Chris was glad when he suggested a brief respite on the way. They stopped near a cave and, unthinking for a moment, Chris curiously followed him inside. It was very dark, and too late she realised that Paul might interpret her going with him as a sign that she had changed her mind about him. That he did, he made clear almost at once, taking her in his arms and crushing her hard against him as his mouth hungrily sought hers.

Chris made a small explosive sound of protest and pushed him away. 'Paul—no—please, don't!' She could not deny that some deep emotional need cried out for fulfilment, but not with Paul . . .

He held her fiercely and his breathing was ragged as he tried to force some response from her, but she gave nothing, and eventually he let her go, defeated, and said a little unkindly, 'Why are you so frigid, Chris? What's the matter with you? Has Africa desiccated your emotions?'

Chris said cautiously, 'I don't want to get involved, Paul, that's all. Not even—this much . . .'

He shook her with annoyance. 'There has to be a reason—why you're not married . . .'

'Paul, it's no business of yours . . .' Chris wrenched away from him. She was angry now. She stumbled towards the entrance. 'I thought there might have been some of those rock paintings you told me about in here, but it's too dark to see properly anyway.' She turned and said back into the gloom where he was just discernible, 'We can go on if you like, or would you rather take me home? I'm sory if I'm spoiling your day—if you got the wrong idea . . .'

Paul slouched after her and as they emerged into the sunshine he slipped an arm around her waist.

'Sorry, Chris. Let's go on to the top. I was a bit boorish . . . forgive?' His smile was a melting one, and Chris sighed and said,

'Of course.'

He looked into her face, perplexed. 'You seem so warm and vital and . . .'

'Don't, Paul . . .' she warned, and as he sighed she felt a twinge of conscience. She shouldn't have come. And she shouldn't have been thinking how much different it would have been if Adrian had held her in his arms. But just as pointless, she thought with a shaft of pain.

She strode on purposefully, anxious to punish herself with hard physical exercise, and this time it was Paul who caught up with her eventually and was breathless. She did not stop until they reached the top of the Pinnacle rock. There, with a strong wind buffeting them, they stood and looked out over the vast panorama of plains with lakes, rivers and scattered settlements stretching to the horizon.

'It's magnificent!' she said, leaning on the railing at the edge of the jagged rocky spur they were on. Paul stood close beside her but did not touch her now.

There had been many enjoyable moments during the day, Chris reflected later, nevertheless she was glad when they arrived back at her house. She knew Paul was disappointed it had not turned out as he had hoped, but to give him his due, during the latter part he had not been churlish, as he might well have been after her rejection in the cave.

In other circumstances she might have invited him in for coffee, or a drink, even a meal, but she decided it might be wise not to. He might still misread her motives.

After she had gone, she made herself a cup of tea and reflected on the day. Most probably he would not ask her out again. She hoped not. She would have to say no if he did. Paul was not the kind of man who would be content just to be a friend. And he was just a little too sure of his charms.

She sighed as she sipped her tea. It was always like this. It always would be.

# CHAPTER SIX

'I HOPE you had a pleasant day yesterday,' Adrian remarked, rather laconically, next morning. 'The weather was perfect.'

Chris was in her room glancing through a medical journal, having arrived at the Centre a little earlier than usual. When he looked in, she raised her head and briefly encountered the dark brown eyes which held, she thought, a speculative expression.

'Yes, it was,' she said, not really answering the first part of the question. She was still wishing she had not gone with Paul. There had been discord because of their separate and different expectations of the day, and she would rather have avoided that since they worked together. She had not seen him yet today and was rather dreading it.

'Paul behaved himself, I trust?' he said, sounding, Chris thought, like a suspicious father.

'That's an unethical question!' she joked. 'I pass!' It was an effort to sound flippant. Was Adrian jealous? she wondered again. Or was it just his protective instinct because he knew Paul's reptuation?

It seemed that he did not appreciate her levity, because he strode into the room and closed the door with a sharp bang. Chris was perched on the edge of her desk and stiffened in alarm, especially when he came straight up to her and placed his hands on her shoulders, preventing her from moving. His expression was unamused. 'Don't go fooling around with Paul,' he warned gratingly.

'Adrian, I'm not . . .' Chris was rigid under his touch, yet she longed to be the opposite, soft and melting in his arms, to feel them folded closely around her, not just resting on her shoulders. This conflict within her made

84

her say irritably, 'It's good of you to be so concerned, Adrian, but really, I am an adult, and . . .'

He did not let her finish. He shook her slightly. 'If you want to fool around with anyone, fool around with me!' He spoke tensely and so softly she hardly heard him. Her answer turned to a gasp of surprise as his mouth covered hers. He ran the tip of his tongue lightly over her lips before crushing them harder, until she felt her will ebbing away and she yielded because it was what she wanted to do. With a sigh he folded her tightly against him and for a moment let passion have its full rein. She was unable to reject him as she had Paul. He drew back and looked searchingly into her face. 'Chris . . .' It was a heartfelt plea and it wrenched her heart agonisingly.

'Adrian—someone might come!' She tried to cover her true feelings with an attempt at outrage.

'To hell!' He touched her temple and traced the line of her cheek. 'Chris, there's still a spark, isn't there—it isn't quite dead, is it?' His facial muscles tautened and a shadow darkened his eyes. 'Chris, do you still think a career is more important than marriage?'

She was startled. 'What do you . . .?' She stopped on a sharp intake of breath, remembering what he meant. That was one of the excuses she had given when she'd ended their relationship.

'Are we really so incompatible?' he demanded, and Chris flinched at the echo of her own words all those years ago when she had used any excuse but the truth.

'Please, Adrian, there's no point in dragging it all up again,' she pleaded. 'You'll only hurt yourself as well as me. I can't believe you've been carrying a torch for me all this time.'

'I didn't believe it either,' he said slowly, 'until I saw you. An apparition at the airport! I thought I was hallucinating, a bad case of jet-lag! I realised later why I'd always side-stepped when there was a possibility of marriage in the offing, avoided getting too involved. Subconsciously I must always have hoped that somewhere, sometime, we'd meet again and sort things out.'

'There's nothing to sort out,' Chris said wearily. 'It's just wishful thinking. If you've been harbouring a dream instead of getting married and having a family, you've been wasting your time. It's time you pulled yourself together and . . .' Her voice wavered on the words that hurt so much to say.

'Not until I'm absolutely convinced I know the real reason why you broke it off,' he said, his eyes intently searching hers, his strong fingers digging into her shoulders to reinforce his determination. 'I never believed the incompatible excuse, or that nonsense about your career. We were about as compatible as two people could ever be, and there was nothing to stop you having a career. I wouldn't have stood in your way. Even having a family needn't have interfered too much. I'd have been only too willing to share . . .'

It was almost more than she could do to hold back from telling him the truth after that. But she resisted the temptation. She had been over it all in her mind so many times and always she had come to the same conclusion. She had been right to break off their relationship, and right not to tell him the real reason why. It was still right.

'Was there someone else?' he asked grittily when she didn't speak. 'Was that the real reason? Was that what you were afraid to tell me, that you'd met someone else?'

'No! There was no-one else,' Chris said. 'It was just too sudden. I-I wasn't ready for such a permanent commitment as marriage. I was frightened of the intensity of our emotions. A strong physical attraction isn't necessarily love.' She averted her eyes. 'Adrian, please . . . It does no good raking over old embers.'

He stoked her ear and ran his fingers around the back of her neck. She shivered involuntarily, knowing he felt her reaction and was encouraged by it, that he was still unconvinced by her words. 'But we're older now, Chris, more sure of our true feelings. We're mature people . . .'

'And we have separate lives now,' she said shakily, hurting more than he would ever know. 'In three months or so I'll be gone from yours again.'

Impetuously, he crushed her close. 'If you do, I'll come with you,' he grated with subdued ferocity. 'You haven't come back into my life like this for me to let you go without a fight a second time. I was too proud to chase after you the first time, especially as I thought there was someone else. But now I know the fire isn't out, and there isn't anyone . . .' He pushed her slightly away, cupped her face in his hands and made her look at him. 'The fire isn't out, Chris,' he stated, emphasising each word with painful clarity. 'You know that, only you won't admit it—yet.'

To prove his point he crushed her lips firmly under his once more and his hands were warm against her flesh through the thin material of her blouse. Skin burning from the contact, Chris steeled herself not to let him sense how strongly her body responded to his, regardless of her mental resistance. She must not let him discover a wider chink in her armour. She must convince him that she had no feelings for him, even if it were untrue. She must somehow convince him that it was all over between them.

She felt guilty because she had failed to achieve that eight years ago. This time she must cure him once and for all, she vowed, clamping her mouth shut under his persuasive onslaught. She must leave him in no doubt that it was over and that his advances were distasteful to her. He must marry someone else and forget her. Rita or Deborah—their names rang mockingly in her ears and set off waves of unbearable jealousy.

She pushed at his shoulders with determination. 'Adrian, please . . .' she muttered, dragging her mouth away. 'Do you want the patients to see?'

His lips were moist and his eyes heavily laden with desire. 'Chris, don't fight me,' he pleaded. 'Remember how it used to be? We can be like that again—happy . . .

You're only hurting yourself this way.'

'No, *you're* hurting me!' she flashed. 'Let me go, Adrian!'

He ignored her pleas. He held her head against his chest, one large hand spread across her fiery cheek and she could feel his heart pounding faster than normal. After a moment he tilted her chin up and looked into her troubled grey eyes. 'I think you still love me, Chris,' he murmured.

She gave a small painful sob. If she told him she loved him, she would have to tell him the other truth as well and at that moment the temptation was strong. She would find happiness with Adrian, as she'd always known she would, but would he in the end achieve happiness with her—deprived of children, the complete family life she knew he wanted and which he was so perfectly made for? She had known eight years ago that she couldn't ask him to make that sacrifice for her, and she mustn't ask him now.

A tap at the door forced Adrian to release her. Carole looked in, glanced from one to the other, her sharp eyes sensing the tension that must still be evident in their faces. Her brows lifted curiously, but all she said was, 'Your first patient's here, Chris. Mrs Gordon.'

Chris, with admirable control, said, 'Send her in, Carole.'

Adrian mumbled something that sounded like, 'See you later,' and left.

With only seconds to compose herself, Chris took a deep breath at the window, clasped her hands tightly together until the knuckles gleamed white, and pushed her shoulders back resolutely. She felt as though she'd been run over by a bulldozer. Was the depth of feeling Adrian had admitted to real, or just a temporary flare-up, a renewal of physical attraction, because her reappearance had awakened memories?

It was so hard to know. But whatever she did she mustn't encourage him. No matter how much she longed to be in his arms, she must resist it. She wouldn't be here much longer. She must keep their relationship friendly and avoid emotional scenes like this one. It wasn't going to be easy, not now.

If her patients that morning noticed that Chris was a little withdrawn or distant from them, they showed no sign of it. But Chris knew she was more detached than she ought to have been. She was functioning on automatic, listening carefully as always to descriptions of symptoms, examining thoroughly, considering carefully before making a diagnosis, but all the time half of her mind was elsewhere.

Her first patient, a middle-aged woman with fibroids whom Chris was referring to a gynaecologist, said, as Chris was writing out the referral, 'How long are you staying in Mount William, Dr Hart?'

'Only until Christmas,' Chris answered.

'I'm sure you'd be very welcome to stay permanently,' said the woman, and with a twinkle in her eyes, 'Can't one of our handsome bachelor doctors persuade you to stay?'

Chris was taken aback, but she managed to laugh. 'I don't think they'd go that far!'

Mrs Gordon said seriously, 'I can't understand why Dr Gilmore—young Dr Adrian, that is—isn't married. He's such a nice kind man, so good with children.'

Chris flinched. 'Yes, he is. But perhaps he's hard to please.'

'Are you hard to please too?' Mrs Gordon asked pointedly.

'Yes, very!' Chris answered lightly as she sealed the envelope. 'Here you are, Mrs Gordon. Ask Sister to make an appointment for you as you go out.' She rose, as did her patient. 'And I'm sure you've got nothing to worry about. A D & C will take care of the problem.'

'I cross my bridges when I come to them,' said the patient cheerfully, and Chris wished more patients had her temperament. Anxiety often caused a great deal of unnecessary anguish. Yet it seemed to be inherent in human nature to worry. As she was worrying about

Adrian.

When Chris had finished seeing her patients that day, she found Rita Vanderhoek in the office, and as Rita wanted to discuss a few matters regarding one or two of Andrew Gilmore's patients who were receiving home visits from the district nurse they went into the lounge for a cup of coffee.

The medical matters were quickly disposed of and they talked of other things for a while. Rita was interested in Chris's experiences in Africa.

'I'd never have the nerve to take on a job like that,' she said regretfully. 'I couldn't bear to leave home.'

'Some people like to travel, others prefer to stay put,' said Chris. 'The world needs both sorts, I guess.'

Rita laughed. She had a warm friendly laugh and she was a popular district nurse. She said, 'Perhaps with me it's because my parents emigrated from Holland years ago. They did the travelling and uprooting. My mother wasn't happy about it but my father wanted to come. After the war he thought it would be a better life for us. I'm the youngest of six children,' she confided with a chuckle. 'I was born here.'

And you'd make an excellent wife for Adrian, Chris thought, with as much charity as she could muster. A much better wife then Deborah, she added to herself. And then thought, 'Mind your own business, Chris Hart!'

Next morning, Rose reminded Chris, 'Your small ops patients start at ten, Chris. The Treatment Room is all set up.' She handed Chris some record cards.

There were three minor surgical procedures to be done which did not require hospitalisation. There was a sebaceous cyst to be removed, also a growth from a finger that was almost certainly non-malignant, and there was an elderly man requiring his ears syringed.

Removal of the cyst was the last, being rather a lengthy operation. It required patience and a steady hand to remove the offending lump without breaking the membrane and perhaps causing infection. It was vital to remove the growth whole so as to avoid the possibility of any later regrowth.

Jill assisted Chris, and as they worked Chris reflected on the plethora of minor operations which were carried out at the clinic in Mali. Most of those would probably be referred to the hospital here, but one needed to exercise a wider range of skills in a country where hospitals were few and far between.

'I'd like you to keep perfectly still,' Chris told her patient, a man in his forties. 'I'm going to give you a local anaesthetic so you won't feel a thing, but if you do, yell and we'll give you a booster shot. This will take a little time, I'm afraid. Let me know if you're feeling too uncomfortable and we'll give you a short break.' The cyst was on the man's back and he was lying on his stomach.

'She'll be right, Doctor,' he said. 'I expect I'll drop off! I'm a shift worker and I'd normally be asleep at this time of the morning.'

'So long as you don't snore!' said Jill. She knew the patient well, and in fact he did not drop off but kept up a fairly continuous conversation with her throughout the operation.

Chris worked quickly and expertly and finally lifted the walnut-sized cyst into the kidney dish Jill held out. 'Now all we have to do is close up the wound,' she said with satisfaction.

'Let's have a look,' said the patient.

Jill showed him the dish and he pulled a face. 'Ugh! Sorry I asked!'

Jill laughed. 'It wasn't as bad as having a tooth pulled, though, was it?'

'Didn't feel a thing,' he agreed, and grinning at Chris, 'It must be the woman's touch. Gentle hands!'

'Dr Hart is pretty deft with a scalpel, it seems,' said a voice that startled Chris. She looked around at Adrian. He had crept in without her noticing.

She felt slightly annoyed. She resented having been

observed without her knowledge, almost as though she was on trial, or being examined. 'How long have you been there?' she demanded curtly.

'A few minutes,' he said.

'Just as well you didn't startle me when I had a scalpel in my hand,' she rejoined, with a touch of asperity.

'I thought you realised I was here,' he said, unrepentant. 'Jill did.'

Chris's lips pursed as she said, 'I was concentrating.' As their eyes locked, her feelings suddenly washed over her in a burning tide. She wasn't angry with him, she was angry with herself for being so hopelessly in love with the man.

Her hands shook now as they had not during the past hour. It was just as well she hadn't sensed his presence, she thought. She made a conscious effort to control herself. This would never do! This wasn't a soap opera on TV with emotional tension between characters in an operating theatre! How ridiculous could you get!

Looking quickly away from the intensity of his gaze, she took the suture from Jill and closed the small wound near the patient's right shoulder blade. Then Jill taped a dressing over the site.

'Keep the dressing on for forty-eight hours,' Chris told her patient, 'and try not to get it wet. You can come back to have the stitches out in about ten days.'

The man sat up and Jill helped him on with his shirt. Adrian did not go, although Chris was wishing he would.

She said, 'The skin might pull a bit for a few days, but you'll only have a tiny scar and that will soon disappear.'

'You're sure it's benign?' The patient asked diffidently, so as not to betray his anxiety.

Chris nodded and said firmly, 'Certain. But we'll have a biopsy done just to make sure, don't worry.' She added, 'How do you feel now? A bit groggy?'

'No, I'm fine,' he said, standing up. He looked a bit pale and was tense still, however.

'Would you like to sit down for a bit?' Chris suggested. 'Sister will fetch you a cup of tea if you like.'

He shook his head. 'My wife's probably waiting for me. I'll be off home, thanks all the same. I'm fine. Thanks a lot. I'm glad to be rid of that door-knob at last.' He grinned. 'At least it'll stop the wife from nagging me about it!'

Jill went out with him, leaving Chris alone with Adrian, who seemed disinclined to leave.

She peeled off her surgical gloves. 'Well, did you learn anything?' she asked flippantly, flashing him a forced smile.

She started to remove her gown, but one of the ties had knotted and when she fumbled with it, he came to her assistance.

'I learned that you're probably a very useful surgeon!'

'One cyst doesn't make a shining career! But I did my BS, naturally.'

They laughed together, all at once companionable as they'd always been in the past, and the tension his sudden appearance had evoked in Chris subsided.

'You didn't mind my watching?' Adrian asked.

'You get used to it, don't you?' Chris said. 'When you're training everybody watches you—doctors have to learn to work with people breathing down their necks all the time.'

His eyes were fixed on her face as though he couldn't drag his gaze away, or he wanted to memorize her features intimately. He said, 'Finished now?'

'Yes.' She glanced at her watch. 'I've just got time for lunch.'

'Let's grab some, then.' He stood aside for her to go out of the room.

As they entered the lounge and Chris made straight for the coffee-urn, Adrian said, 'Mother would like you to come to lunch on Sunday, if you're free. Rachel and family are coming over. She's keen for them to meet you.'

Chris raised her eyebrows. 'All this notoriety! I'm embarrassed!' She would go, of course. She could not offend the Gilmores, not after they had been so kind to her, but she really would have rather not.

They sat down, Adrian a little too close for Chris's comfort, and she wished she'd chosen a chair instead of the couch.

'You don't really mind, do you?' Adrian said seriously, sensing her reluctance but not the real reason for it. 'I think you'll like Rachel. She's a lot like Mother. The twins are a bit of a handful, though. Imagine, two sets of the little monsters!' He chuckled, and his affection for his sister's family was very plain.

'I'm sure your mother can cope,' Chris said.

'You'll come?'

'Yes, I'd like to. But I hope your mother doesn't feel she has to keep taking pity on me because I'm living alone.'

He placed a hand lightly on her thigh. It was a reassuring gesture, that was all, but Chris's deepest senses reacted to it. 'Chris, surely you've heard of good old Australian country hospitality, or have you been away too long? My mother was a farmer's daughter!'

She had spent almost every Sunday at the Gilmores since she had arrived, Chris thought, as she was dressing on Sunday morning. And it had always been enjoyable. She liked the Gilmores very much, but she had to admit that painful though it sometimes was, being with Adrian off duty was also, in its way, a precious time which she would not otherwise have enjoyed. Thinking of how much she loved being with him, she suddenly allowed the treacherous thought to enter her mind that perhaps, after all, a new relationship between them might not be so impossible. She was sure she knew what Adrian would say if she told him the truth, that it didn't matter . . . But later? That was her dilemma and had been from the beginning. What about later?

She pulled on a grey pleated skirt and deep purple

sweater, as despite the recent warm weather the day promised to be cool again. She combed her sleek dark hair into place, taking a good look at herself in the mirror as she did so. I won't see thirty again, she thought ruefully, and it would be nice to be married . . . To Adrian . . . only to him . . . She looked away quickly, afraid that the longing reflected in her eyes would persuade her to do what she had always felt in her heart would be selfish and wrong.

Chris took to Rachel as soon as they were introduced. The only trouble was that Rachel seemed convinced that there was a blossoming relationship between Chris and her brother. Janet had fuelled that notion, Chris was certain.

The tall, brown-haired Rachel Jackson bore a strong resemblance to her brother, but she had a less reserved nature. She was all bounce and energy and lively chatter, and Chris thought at once how popular she must have been on the wards when she was nursing. Rachel had the disposition to make even the most seriously ill patients feel optimistic. And yet, Chris thought, she seemed also the kind of girl who would not stand for any nonsense.

Their first real opportunity to talk came when Chris and Rachel volunteered to do the washing up after lunch.

Rachel said, 'I hope you're going to graduate from locum to local, Chris. I don't think Dad ought to take on a full practice again, do you?'

'No, I don't,' agreed Chris, 'but I suppose that's really a decision for his doctors.'

'And Mum!' Rachel pulled a face. 'Dad's very stubborn. So's Adrian. They're very much alike—very close too. That's why Adrian rushed home.' She glanced around at Chris, who was studiously wiping cutlery. 'Well, is there any chance of your staying?'

Chris had to say, 'Didn't Adrian tell you I'm going back to Africa in the New Year?'

'He mentioned it, but I thought he was hell-bent on

getting you to change your mind!'

'He wouldn't want to do that,' Chris said carefully.

Rachel shrugged. 'Then I must have got the wrong end of the stick.' She laughed. 'I usually do.' Her look was now one of disappointment and puzzlement. 'I know I've only met you today, but I agree with Mum, you seem just right for Adrian. I was watching you at lunchtime—you fit in with all of us so . . . so naturally.' She laughed again apologetically. 'Sorry if that sounds selfish, but it's nice if a family gets on well with its in-laws. My brother Philip's wife is a pain . . .' She broke off. 'Oops, I shouldn't say things like that!'

Chris smiled at her candour, but was disturbed by the part concerning her and Adrian. She said, 'It's a nice compliment, but I'm afraid there's no burgeoning relationship between Adrian and me.'

'Pity. I'm scared stiff he'll go and marry someone like that awful Deborah Leigh. She'd be worse than Val, Philip's wife! Oh, I daresay she's nice enough—Deborah, I mean—but I can't see Adrian being happy with someone like her. Now you . . .'

'You're very fond of your brother, aren't you?' Chris put in quickly as she stacked the plates where Rachel had shown her.

'Yes. We're a close family really, even though we're all a bit scattered now.' Rachel let the water out of the sink and above its gurgling said casually, 'Don't you want to settle down and have a family, Chris?'

It was blunt. Rachel was that kind of person, but Chris did not resent it. Her stomach tightened, however, and tears welled briefly in her eyes. Fortunately Rachel began to wipe the sink around and didn't notice her emotion.

Chris injected control into her answer. 'I haven't thought seriously about it,' she said. 'So far the possibility hasn't arisen.'

Rachel said, 'It'd rise like tomorrow's sun if you so much as hinted to Adrian, I'm sure.' She paused to regard Chris closely. 'I'm sure he's in love with you.

Are you quite sure you feel nothing for him?'

Rachel was too nice, too fond of her brother, for Chris to take offence. She said slowly, 'I like Adrian very much—but only as a friend. Our lives and careers would scarcely be compatible.'

'Compromise,' said Rachel, 'is the only answer to life's little dilemmas. Look at me. I was set to be Director of Nursing at one of the biggest private hospitals in Melbourne when along came this irresistible dentist who wouldn't budge from dear old deadly dull Ballarat!'

'Is it really so dull?' Chris queried with a laugh.

'With two sets of twins hardly dull!' admitted Rachel. 'But—well, it isn't Melbourne.' She added drily, 'Don't get me wrong, though. I love living there and we're only a couple of hours' drive from Melbourne. When the kids are older things will be different, they're a bit of a tic at the moment. I never intended to have five. Camille was to be the last, and I nearly died when I found I was having twins again!'

Chris laughed. 'Two sets was overdoing it a bit, I suppose!'

'Downright irresponsible,' said Rachel. 'Dan complains that he'll have to open a string of surgeries to pay for their education!'

'But at least you won't have to pay their dental bills,' Chris observed.

Rachel chuckled. 'Sure, it's an ill wind . . .' She looked sharply at Chris again. 'Don't you want to have children, Chris?'

It was tempting to confide in Rachel, but Chris knew she couldn't trust her not to tell Adrian. She took a deep breath. 'I have a lot to do with children in my work. It's very satisfying work.'

Rachel nodded. 'It must be.' She went on, 'I was never crazy about babies, I admit. I preferred climbing trees to dressing dolls. I could have lived without them, but I love them, though, the little monsters.' She paused and said thoughtfully after a moment, 'I wasn't joking when I said that about feeling irresponsible. I sometimes feel very selfish for adding more to a world in which there are more than enough starving . . .'

'You couldn't help having twins,' said Chris.

Rachel grinned. 'I console myself that at least it wasn't triplets or quads!' She cocked an ear. 'Sounds of silence. I wonder what they're all up to. Not mischief, I hope. Dan's supposed to be keeping his fatherly eye on them.'

'I'll go and see,' offered Chris.

In the living room doorway she stopped, her face breaking into a broad grin. Andrew Gilmore lay on the couch, fast asleep. Dan Jackson was sprawled in an armchair with Camille, his three-year-old daughter, on his lap, both also asleep.

In another armchair lay Adrian, a slumbering five-year-old twin boy in the crook of each arm. He stirred as though sensing Chris's presence and opened his eyes.

'I was telling them a story,' he whispered. 'It must have been very boring!'

Chris chuckled. 'It certainly must have been for the storyteller to drop off too! I think Janet's superb cooking had more to do with it, though.'

'My right arm is numb,' Adrian complained, shifting slightly. 'Can you take Danny?'

Chris lifted the soundly sleeping five-year-old. 'I'll put him in the spare bedroom,' she suggested.

She was gently lowering the child on to a bed when Adrian entered with the other twin, James, and deposited him on the second bed.

Chris jumped when his fingers brushed the back of her neck as she was still bending over the sleeping Danny. His fingertips massaged the small hollow at the nape and sent electric shocks coursing through her.

'I feel like some fresh air,' he whispered. 'Like to take the dogs for a walk?'

'Might be a good idea,' she murmured, but didn't expect him to appreciate the irony.

She moved aside, but not before Rachel had come in

and had noticed Adrian's intimate gesture. His sister's eyes narrowed suspiciously and Chris knew she would regard the intimacy as significant.

'What an unsociable lot!' Rachel exclaimed, adding, 'Aren't they sweet when they're asleep!' She jerked her head towards one of the other bedrooms. 'Mum's sleeping it off in her room with the babies, so I think I might as well have forty winks too. What are you two going to do?'

'We're taking the dogs for a walk,' said Adrian.

Rachel gave Chris what could only be described as a hopeful smile.

They went out the back way, along an overgrown path down the garden, and scrambled under a wire fence. There was a track across the paddocks beyond, which led in the general direction of a belt of bush. The two spaniels gambolled on ahead of them delightedly, obviously on familiar terrain.

A few sheep were grazing in the paddocks, but the dogs did not go near them. The tiny white lambs which had dotted the landscape when Chris had arrived in Mount William were bigger and greyer now, but still frolicking with the liveliness of youth. Magpies were chattering somewhere in the distance. It was a peaceful rural scene with the mountains as a backdrop and a sky that was stainless blue between the snowball clouds.

'Nice day,' remarked Adrian.

'Beautiful day,' Chris agreed, aware of a mounting tension between them.

They walked on in silence until they came to the dam, which was ringed by trees. Adrian made straight for a large fallen log while the dogs fossicked happily along the bank. They sat down and watched a heron stalking along the edge of the water and swallows gathering mud for their nests.

'Where are they taking it?' Chris asked, intrigued.

Adrian pointed out some distant sheds and a windmill. 'Over there probably. They come back to the same nest sites every year and never lose their way.

Thousands and thousands of miles. Remarkable, isn't it?'

'Some people say migration is just blind instinct. But there's intelligence too,' Chris said. 'I'm sure of it.'

They made short spurts of inconsequential conversation for some minutes and Chris felt the old rapport and companionableness they'd enjoyed years before sweeping over her in a tide, enmeshing her more strongly than ever.

At last Adrian said, 'We'd better make tracks. Mother will be thinking about afternoon tea any minute!'

'I hope she won't expect us to eat anything!' Chris patted her stomach with laughter.

'You don't know the Gilmores,' Adrian said, rising from his log. 'We're all born with hollow legs.' He held out his hand to Chris and, forgetting herself, she took it. He kept hold of it after she was standing and she did not pull free. Some strange compulsion made her leave her fingers resting within the firm grasp of his and treacherously the selfish thought surfaced again— maybe . . . Her heart beat faster as she read only too clearly the expression in his eyes.

He was waiting for her to move, she could feel it in the tenseness of his fingers. He wanted her in his arms, but he wanted her to make the first move. For a long moment their eyes held and silently they engaged in a battle of wills. But Chris knew how much she wanted to fall into his arms, how much she wanted to have and to hold, for ever, she might not be proof against his persuasion, and for his sake as well as her own, she must hold out against him.

With a supreme effort of will she dragged her eyes away, abruptly jerked her hand from his grasp and stepped purposefully towards the track leading back to the house.

Adrian said nothing. He just called to the dogs who came gambolling up. When he said, 'Home!' they streaked off ahead of him and Chris.

Chris tried to keep up a light conversation as they walked, but it was hard. She dared not look at Adrian, and when they accidently brushed against each other, every nerve in her body jumped at the contact.

They were almost back at the fence at the rear of the Gilmores' garden when he said, 'You haven't been down to Melbourne since you've been here. Don't you want to visit your folks?'

'Yes, of course, but they've been away on holiday. Mother and Dad went off on a cruise a few days after I came up here. As a matter of fact, they're back now, and I hope to go down one weekend soon. It's Mother's birthday on the last Sunday of the month.'

'The last Sunday . . .' he repeated. 'Well, that's a happy coincidence.' He fished in his pocket for a small diary. 'That's the weekend of my medical dinner.' He slid her a questioning look. 'Would you like to drive down with me?'

'A lift, you mean?'

'Why not? No point in us both driving, is there? And you can do me a favour and come to the dinner with me. It's on the Friday night. All medical people. Probably a few you'll know. And wives and husbands, of course.'

Can't Deborah make it? Chris was thinking. Or Rita? She was remembering the phone-call in Deborah's shop and something about a weekend in Melbourne. Perhaps now Deborah couldn't go. She could hardly ask, so she said doubtfully, 'I don't know . . .'

Adrian regarded her intently as they paused at the fence. 'You'll still have the whole weekend for your family.'

'But what about you? Did you intend to stay down the whole two days?'

'As a matter of fact, yes. There are one or two friends I haven't seen for some time.' It didn't sound too convincing to Chris.

'Well, so long as you're not organising it just to suit me . . .'

She was sure he was, and he didn't deny it. 'I'd be

grateful if you'd come to dinner with me,' he said.

'All right,' Chris said. 'If you're sure . . .'

He lifted up the wires and she scrambled through into the Gilmores' garden. As Adrian had predicted, afternoon tea was ready. Everyone except the babies was now awake and, it seemed, ravenous again. Chris and Adrian collected some knowing looks on their return and Chris knew she was foolish to have gone for a walk with him alone. They were bound to regard it as significant. She had the feeling they were talking about her and Adrian and stopped the moment they walked in. It was flattering to know she would be welcome in the family, and the Gilmores would be a lovely family to belong to, she thought wistfully, if only . . . The treacherous thought surfaced again that maybe it *was* possible.

But presently, when Adrian began to amuse the children by giving them rides on all fours around the living room, up the passage and in and out of the bedrooms, pretending to be a horse, a camel, or a donkey or whatever animal the children demanded, Chris knew that she couldn't, mustn't entertain even for a moment the possibility of marrying Adrian.

He loved children. That was obvious from the way he fooled around with his sister's brood. She listened to him imitating the sounds of the animals he was impersonating, and the hoots of delight from the young ones, and her heart ached. To deny him children of his own because she so selfishly coveted his love would be wickedness.

She began to wish she hadn't let herself be inveigled into going down to Melbourne with him.

# CHAPTER SEVEN

CHRIS'S parents were delighted that she was coming home for her mother's birthday. Ellen Hart was also avidly interested when she learned that her daughter would be going out to dinner on the Friday night with Adrian, but she knew better than to quiz her too closely about it. She simply crossed her fingers and said to Chris's father, 'I do hope they're getting together again.'

As time would be short, Chris and Adrian decided to dress for dinner before leaving Mount William. Chris hurried home on Friday afternoon as soon as she could get away from the Centre and quickly showered and changed into a pearl grey silk dress with a softly moulded bodice, full long sleeves and a draped skirt. Despite her uneasiness over Adrian, she was looking forward to the dinner. She was just slipping on a black velvet jacket when he rang the bell.

'Mmm—very chic,' he commented flatteringly at his first sight of her as she opened the door to him. He bent and kissed her cheek, murmuring, 'You make me wish this was a rather different sort of weekend!'

She stepped back, caught the twinkle in his eye and said flippantly, 'Adrian! Think what your mother would say!'

'She'd say I ought to marry you!'

To hide her sudden flush, Chris bent to pick up her overnight case. So did Adrian. Their hands collided and he linked her fingers in his. 'Chris . . .'

Chris jumped back and shook her head vigorously. 'Don't, Adrian . . .'

He looked crushed. 'All right. I know where I stand.' He regarded her quizzically. 'You seem different somehow, Chris, more withdrawn than you used to be, as though—Chris, has someone hurt you?'

She bit her lip. This was no way to start the evening.

103

'I think we'd better go,' she said, 'or we'll be late for your dinner.'

He let the question ride and on the long drive down to Melbourne, Chris carefully guided the conversation away from personal matters and firmly on to medical topics. She had been reading an article in a medical journal about a new and controversial treatment for peptic ulcers, and as Adrian had also read it, this provided the basis for a lively discussion which lasted most of the way.

Soon they were driving through Melton and the city skyline came into view just as it was getting dark. They were only a few minutes late when they crossed the river at Hawthorn and made their way to the venue.

There were more people at the dinner than Chris had expected. She saw a few faces she knew, some from the old days, some she had met recently while she was working at the South City General again. There were friendly greetings and Adrian introduced her to other people. She began to relax. At dinner she and Adrian were seated at a round table for eight, with a gynaecologist and her radiologist husband, an oncologist and his wife who was a nurse, as also was the wife of the cardio-vascular specialist. One woman was a Director of Nursing at a private hospital and the other had given up work as a Theatre Sister to have a family.

'I'm going back as soon as I can, though,' she told Chris, 'and meanwhile Eric keeps me up to date as best he can on OR technology.'

'Technology in medicine certainly moves fast,' Chris agreed.

When the waiter brought the menus, Adrian, indicating Chris, said, 'This lady is a vegetarian. I've already spoken to the management.'

The waiter nodded. 'Very good, sir. That's no problem.'

Chris glanced at Adrian gratefully. He was always so considerate, always smoothing the way for people, friends as well as patients.

During the early part of the meal, people talked more to

those on either side of them than as a group. Chris found herself in deep discussion with the cardio-vascular specialist, while Adrian seemed to have found common ground—wine—with the gynaecologist, whose family apparently owned a vineyard in Western Australia.

By the time dessert and coffee had been served, the conversation had broadened to round-table discussions and there were some lively exchanges on the effects of diet on disease and health in general. Cholesterol, sugar, alcohol and fibre all came under scrutiny.

The subject seemed to be exhausted when the oncologist's wife, who was DON at a private hospital, suddenly said into a momentary pool of silence, 'You're a vegetarian, Dr Hart. Is it for health or religious reasons?' Her finely pencilled eyebrows rose fractionally and her look was slightly provocative.

Chris was used to the loaded question and answered quietly, 'Neither, Mrs Herford. It's because I'm opposed to cruelty to animals. It isn't necessary and it isn't moral.'

Her words, though quietly spoken, seemed to her to echo loudly around the entire room, but that was fancy. Only the profound silence around her table made it seem so. Every eye was suddenly turned on her and Chris didn't dare look at Adrian, who was no doubt writhing in embarrassment.

Chris let her own eyes move from face to face with a kind of fascination. It was almost as though she'd said something lewd. It wasn't the first time she'd been asked the question, of course. Reactions were usually mixed, ranging from the patronising to the sympathetic, from mildly mocking to downright hostile. Sometimes people were eager to discuss the issue, which usually meant eager to justify themselves, but mostly she had found people preferred to draw the blinds on the topic and go on to something less controversial.

She waited for a safe topic to be hurriedly introduced, but it didn't happen. Instead, Mrs Herford, with a faintly derisory smile, said, 'Well, I'm an animal lover, always have been, but I can't see what's wrong with eating meat.'

Her voice had the familiar defensive tone.

Chris drew in a deep breath. She did not relish being the focus of attention or at the centre of a controversial discussion, but to retreat would be cowardly, despite the fact that experience had taught her that cruelty to animals as a dinner table topic was more likely to inflame passions than religion or politics.

'You don't presumably eat the animals you love, though?' Chris queried, thinking she might as well be provocative.

'Roast cat and devilled dog, I hear, go down very well in some cultures,' said a jocular male voice from the other side of the table. It was the radiologist.

Chris flinched. Self-conscious jocularity was as much a sign, she believed, as hostility, that a conscience was being uncomfortably pricked.

Mrs Herford exclaimed, 'That's ridiculous! Pets are one thing, they're domesticated. Farm animals are bred for food. They're different.'

'In what way?' Chris asked mildly.

Mrs Herford looked momentarily surprised at the question. She blustered, 'Well, they're bred for food, as I said, have been for thousands of years.'

'But they still have the same capacity to suffer as domestic pets or any other animals,' Chris pointed out. 'And today cruelty to animals raised for food exists on a scale never before imagined. The horrors of factory farming are fairly recent.'

The heart specialist argued, 'No worse than life in the wild where life is a perpetual struggle for survival and every animal lives in fear of its life.'

Chris met his gaze unflinchingly. 'Wouldn't you prefer that to a life of close confinement? Wouldn't you rather have your freedom, however hazardous, to lifelong imprisonment under unnatural conditions? I don't believe it's humane to imprison hens in cages or to use artificial lighting and chemically treated food to induce them to lay more, or to mutilate their beaks. I don't believe it's humane to keep pigs in pens so small they're unable to turn around, and perpetually pregnant, unable to fulfil all their natural functions, just so humans can have bacon and eggs for breakfast. Good nutrition doesn't require cruelty.'

The heart specialist enquired, 'You approve of free-range poultry and pigs?'

'As an alternative to factory-farming, of course,' said Chris. 'But the animals still have to be killed in the end.' She added, 'Have you ever been to an abattoir?'

The distaste that instantly entered every face betrayed their squeamishness at even the thought of it.

'Yes, but Nature's cruel,' said Mrs Herford dismissively. 'You can't change that.'

'I agree, Nature can be cruel,' agreed Chris, 'which is all the more reason, surely, for humans, who have a choice, not to be. Carnivorous animals have no choice. They have to kill to eat. We humans can choose, to be cruel or not. I really don't believe any of us wants to be cruel. Most of us let someone else do the dirty work nowadays because basically we're squeamish about killing, even animals. And we as a profession are healers, not killers.'

There was an uneasy stirring, but Mrs Herford was still on the defensive. 'Well, so far I know, there are laws controlling the treatment of animals.'

'Yes, there are,' agreed Chris, and caught a sidelong look from Adrian, whose expression she anxiously tried to read. How he must be cursing her for this! To her surprise, there was not the reproach she had expected in his eyes, nor disapproval, nor even an urgent plea to wind up the conversation. What she saw was surely the warmth of encouragement. It surprised her because although he had previously shown sympathy for her views, she nevertheless had assumed he did not entirely agree with her.

His encouraging look helped her to go on, 'Unfortunately, most laws applying to farm animals are only as humane as they're cost-effective. And they're discriminatory. There are laws applying to pet animals that don't apply to farm animals. There are only voluntary codes of practice for food animals. You can, for instance, confine pigs and hens and other food animals for the whole of their reproductive lives in conditions which it would be illegal to inflict on a dog or cat. For some illogical reason we regard pets as different from other animals.'

The gynaecologist chipped in, 'But if we stopped farming animals, Dr Hart, the rural community would collapse.' She smiled a little teasingly. 'And think of all those millions of cows and sheep, pigs and chickens running around loose in the countryside. It would be an environmental disaster!'

There was a ripple of laughter, and when it subsided, Chris said, 'As mass overnight conversion to compassionate vegetarianism is highly unlikely, Dr Morland, I don't think you need to worry. Such a change would inevitably be gradual, and would therefore have a gradual economic effect, just as other social changes have had. We don't, for example, still send children to work in the mines and mills because it's economic, do we? We regard slavery as immoral despite its economic advantages. We've made moral as well as material progress despite the pressures of so-called economic necessity.'

Chris glanced at Adrian again, apologetically, but he just nodded as though agreeing with her. But I must sound awfully pompous, she thought, still looking for disapproval behind his quirky smile. So far he had not entered the discussion, which surely meant he disagreed with her, but of course he was too loyal to do so publicly. This must be bringing home to him, though, just how incompatible they now were.

The heart surgeon, who Chris had expected would try to change the subject, surprised her by saying, 'I presume, Dr Hart, that you also have radical views on the use of animals in medical research?' His gimlet eyes challenged her. She remembered him from her intern days, but of course he didn't recall her. He'd always been a regular tartar, although his bark had been worse than his bite. He was regarding her more tolerantly than unkindly now.

What am I doing here? Chris thought suddenly. How

did I get embroiled in this? She fought down a desperate urge to run and clasped her hands tightly in her lap, determined not to panic. All at once warm fingers closed over hers and squeezed reassuringly. She felt a surge of love and gratitude towards Adrian for this gesture. With his support she could face anything.

'Yes,' she answered boldly. 'I am against painful and unnecessary experiments on animals.' It hardly mattered now what the others said or thought. All that mattered was for Adrian to be on her side, even though that was all they could share.

There was a murmur around the table. Mr Cochrane smiled indulgently. 'I'm sure we would all be against cruelty in principle, Dr Hart, and do our best to ensure that none occurred, but you must agree that medicine could not have made the immense strides it has without experimentation on animals. Drugs must be tested for safety, surgical procedures perfected.'

'I would suggest, sir,' Chris replied politely, 'that if our ethics had precluded the use of animals, as they preclude humans, even greater progress might have been made. Animals do not, as we all know, always give results that can be reliably extrapolated to humans. Look at drug toxicity testing—thalidomide is a classic example, but there are others, as I'm sure you're all aware. And a great deal of animal experimentation, even for so-called medical purposes, is frivolous, resulting in little or no benefit to humans at all.'

Nobody disagreed, but the gynaecologist interposed incredulously, 'So what's your alternative? We can't just let people die!'

'In spite of animal experiments and new discoveries, new cures, people still do die, often of preventable diseases. It might be more economical and more effective to shift the emphasis on to prevention rather than cure. And I would like to see more time, money and brains diverted into researching alternative testing methods, such as techniques using computers and tissue culture, and maybe developing other techniques as yet unknown to us.'

She glanced around the table, and smiled hopefully. 'I'm not suggesting an overnight revolution in this area either. I simply happen to think that if we acknowledged that our methods are cruel, and that if the will existed to find alternatives, alternatives would be found— eventually.'

A few sceptical looks greeted her remarks, but Chris was used to being the dissenter.

Dr Morland said, 'Do you object to experiments which are conducted humanely, under anaesthetic?'

Chris said firmly, 'For the reasons I've just stated, yes. But until there's a change of attitude, we should at least be humane in our treatment of animals in the laboratory. Unfortunately, we are not always so. There's insufficient supervision by outsiders. Anaesthetics are not always used because in some experiments to use them would alter results. Then there are psychological experiments, often subjecting animals to diabolical cruelties.' She added drily, 'Sometimes the aim of experimentation seems to be no more than to prove something we already know, or to gain prestige by publishing findings in scientific and medical journals. The usefulness of the results is often very doubtful indeed.'

As her voice rose in scorn, she felt Adrian's fingers squeeze hers again, and this time she felt she detected some alarm. Poor Adrian! It was unfair subjecting him to this, but she had to stand by what she believed.

'Strong words,' muttered Dr Herford, raising his eyebrows disapprovingly at her, as though she were still a raw medical student.

To Chris's surprise, Adrian joined in. 'I agree with Chris that a lot of expensive medical research is frivolous, repetitive and unnecessary. When I was overseas recently, I saw many things that jolted my conscience. There's an element of big business in the research fields that leaves little room for humanitarianism towards humans, let alone concern for animals.'

Chris was so touched she wanted to weep. She hadn't expected such firm support from him. A flood of love went out from her to him and if, as she glanced at him, he saw it in her eyes, then it couldn't be helped. She held his hand tightly. Perhaps deep down, he did share her views after all. For a moment all she could think of was being at one with Adrian, loving him for ever, despite the reasons why she had believed it impossible.

The gynaecologist brought her back to earth, saying, 'I agree, you have a point, Dr Gilmore. I can't say I agree with everything Dr Hart has said, but I certainly am opposed to frivolous experimentation, and I'm against testing consumer produces such as cosmetics, toiletries and household cleaners and suchlike on animals. The LD 50 and Draize tests are particularly cruel, and unnecessary.'

'Please . . .' put in the heart surgeon's wife, 'do we have to talk about this over dinner?'

Chris's grey eyes flashed. 'Yes! The more it's talked about the more enlightened we, as a community, may become. And as doctors we may even discover we can be of greater benefit to humanity through being compassionate towards animals as well!'

'Dr Hart is something of a lateral thinker, it seems,' said Mr Cochrane with a touch of sarcasm.

Adrian entered the fray again. 'It seems logical to suggest that instead of artificially inducing in animals malignant tumours, heart disease, strokes and other fatal conditions, many of which are self-inflicted in humans through diet, lifestyle and other factors, we might benefit humanity more by concentrating more of our efforts on educating the community in prevention to disease. This is exactly what we were talking about earlier, isn't it?'

He glanced at Chris and grateful tears filled her eyes. She blinked them away rapidly, hoping no one would notice.

'But we mustn't become too emotional about it,' insisted Mrs Herford.

'Why not?' said Chris bluntly. 'Compassion is the finest emotion there is. And it's what our profession is all about. But we're often accused of losing sight of humanitarian values. Maybe we need more emotion, not less.'

There was a brief silence, then Mr Cochrane drawled laconically, in an obvious attempt to demolish her, 'Would you, Dr Hart, refuse medication for yourself, that might save your life, because animals had been involved in its development?' He added, 'And of course it goes without saying that you would not withhold treatment from your patients, whatever your views?'

Chris answered quietly, 'I think that was a little uncalled for, Mr Cochrane, but since you ask, the answer is no, I probably wouldn't have the courage to refuse, but my weakness is not an argument in favour of continuing cruelty, it's an argument in favour of seeking alternatives, so that we shouldn't even be confronted with a choice.' She paused and looked him straight in the eye. 'I'm a doctor, Mr Cochrane, and I would have expected you to take it for granted that my patients always come first.'

There was a slightly embarrassed silence. Chris, to her surprise, felt that perhaps for the first time there was genuine sympathy for her. Mr Cochrane had gone just a little too far.

It was Mrs Herford who finally said in a slightly jocular tone, 'Well, it's an imperfect world we live in. I'm all for preventive medicine. And we all do what we can . . .'

Her husband enquired, 'How long have you been a vegetarian, Dr Hart?'

'Several years.'

He smiled. 'And a convert is always amongst the most dedicated to the cause.'

Adrian put in, 'There's a lot of food for thought in what Chris has been saying. Perhaps we should stop sometimes and think about where we and our profession are heading.'

Chris shot him another swift look of gratitude. Yet underneath he was probably cursing her for embroiling a perfectly amiable dinner party in such a contentious discussion. She hadn't started it, but perhaps she had sounded off rather vehemently. She hadn't meant to lecture them, but it was something she believed in strongly . . . She sighed. If she'd ruined their evening, she was sorry, but there was nothing she could do about it now.

And there was so much more she could have said! There was so much she was quite sure even they were ignorant about. But you didn't alter attitudes by beating people over the head with clubs. You dropped pebbles in pools and hoped the ripples would widen. She smiled ruefully to herself. She'd lobbed a few rocks into this pool, she feared.

For a moment, her innate sense of good manners tempted her to apologise for being so forceful in her views, but she thought the better of it. Why should she apologise? Someone mentioned the weather and small talk began around the table again. Adrian gave her hand a hard squeeze before he took his away. He smiled directly into her eyes and she loved him more than ever because of what he had done for her tonight.

Driving home to her parents' house later, Adrian suddenly chuckled and said to the now rather subdued Chris, 'I never knew you were such a little firebrand, Chris!'

There had been silence between them since they had left the reception centre and she'd thought that perhaps he was angry with her after all, that he'd only lent his support because she was his guest.

'I'm sorry! I did rather thump the tub, didn't I?'

'You caused a certain amount of discomfort!'

'I didn't mean to embarrass you in front of your friends,' she said regretfully.

'Don't be silly, Chris! They aren't friends—I only know two of them casually, and like you hadn't met the others before.' He glanced at her with admiration as they halted at traffic lights. 'It doesn't hurt anyone to have their complacency shaken occasionally. You spoke from the head as well as the heart.' He chuckled. 'There isn't often a dissident in the camp! You'll be talked about for weeks!'

'Dr Gilmore's crank friend?' Chris murmured wryly. She took a deep breath. She felt drained. She hated argument. 'I'd rather they discussed the issue than me.'

'Some may,' he suggested. 'It's an issue we all try to avoid, I'm afraid. There are so many difficulties.' He added apologetically, 'We're not all as dogmatic as that bunch, I hope.'

'It was very kind of you to support me,' Chris answered softly.

He glanced at her, half-smiling, but said nothing. The lights changed and the car surged forward. Chris suddenly felt that in some strange way, this evening had brought them closer together than they had ever been, and certainly there was more accord between them than at any time since her return. It was almost, she thought, with rapidly beating heart, the closeness they'd enjoyed eight years ago. All too soon they were back at her parents' house. Chris invited him in for coffee but Adrian refused.

'It's late and I don't want to disturb your parents or keep my friends up,' he said. 'Have a nice weekend, Chris.'

'You too. Don't forget you're coming to tea on Sunday,' she reminded him.

'I won't. I'm looking forward to meeting your parents again then.'

Chris half wished he wasn't, because she knew that her parents were jumping to the same conclusions she was sure Janet and Andrew were. The conclusions that she herself didn't dare dwell on . . . or did she?

They were standing in the shadowy porch and Chris's key was in the door. She said, 'Thank you for inviting me, Adrian. I'm sorry if I spoiled it for you.'

He gripped her shoulders. 'You didn't spoil anything, you little idiot. I was proud of you!'

'You don't have to flatter me. Or agree with me!'

'Chris.' Adrian pulled her into his arms and kissed her slowly and searchingly. It seemed just a natural part of his embrace for his hands to caress her breasts and his thighs to press hard against her. For a moment she thought of nothing but the bliss of being in his arms and responsive to his touch, a closeness they had once enjoyed and that had been so long denied. After the tensions of the past couple of hours she wanted nothing more than the comfort he offered, and she accepted it hungrily. When he raised his lips at last, he said, 'When you kiss me like that, Chris, I begin to think . . .'

Chris, suddenly ashamed of her weakness, pushed him away. 'You mustn't get any wrong ideas . . .' It was hard to sound cold when he had warmed her so thoroughly.

'Why not, Chris?' he said half angrily. 'We used to . . .'

Why not? echoed every pore in her body, crying out with longing for him. Why not? But the small insistent voice of her conscience still made her hold back. 'Because I'm going back to Mali in a couple of months' time.'

'You're so dedicated,' he answered, faintly scathing.

Chris didn't answer. She didn't wnt to provoke another argument. And she must not encourage him to take advantage of her weakness.

'Goodnight, Adrian,' she said, turning her key in the door.

He detained her with strong fingers about her wrist. 'Chris, come back to the car for a minute—I want to talk . . .'

The glow of the street light was enough to show her his expression, but even if it hadn't, she would have known from the tension in his fingers how highly charged his emotions were. And her own were at flashpoint. It wasn't easy to say with forced indifference, 'Haven't we had enough talk for one night? I'm tired, Adrian. It's very late. I'll go in now if you don't mind.'

His hand dropped from her wrist and he stepped back. 'All right. Goodnight, Chris.' He turned and stomped down the path, and she heard the car door slam and the gears clash with tears in her eyes.

# CHAPTER EIGHT

'I'D LIKE you to see Mrs Forster, Chris,' Rita Vanderhoek said, 'as soon as you can.' The district nurse's face was anxious. 'She's the elderly asthmatic, one of Dr Gilmore's patients—Dr Gilmore senior, I mean, of course.'

'Yes, I remember,' Chris said.

Rita went on, 'Her condition seems to have deteriorated rather rapidly during the past week or so.'

'What anti-spasmodic does she use—Ventolin?'

Rita nodded. 'I happened to arrive yesterday as she was having an attack. The wheezing was very pronounced and she was in rather obvious distress. Her face was somewhat congested and there was cyanosis. The inhaler wasn't readily to hand and she was panicking a bit.'

'The Ventolin was effective, though?'

Rita said anxiously, 'Not as immediate as I thought it should have been. That's why I wondered if you could go along and look at her.'

'You think she might need to be hospitalised?'

'I am a bit worried about emphysema,' admitted Rita, 'but getting her into hospital will be a problem. She's a very independent old lady.'

'I'll call and see her this afternoon after surgery,' Chris promised. 'Can you come along too then, Rita?'

'Yes, of course.' Rita looked relieved and smiled warmly. Chris, with a sudden pang, was reminded of what a highly suitable wife she would make for Adrian.

It was a few days after the trip to Melbourne and she had seen very little of him since. She still felt guilty about the controversial discussion that had erupted over the dinner table and she was sure he must be wishing he hadn't taken her. Loyalty had forced him to support her. Adrian was not the sort of man who would have stood by and seen his guest take a lone stand amongst strangers all too

116

eager to shoot her views down in flames and label her a crank.

He had come to her parents' house for tea that Sunday and he had got along so well with them that it had been hard to get away. Chris's parents had met him only briefly eight years before, from time to time when he had called for Chris, but they greeted him like an old friend and it was obvious to her that they were certain there was a renewed relationship.

Chris was in the bedroom collecting her overnight bag when her mother came in. 'Chris darling,' she whispered, 'I'm so glad!'

'What about?' Chris asked, but her mother's expression was answer enough.

'You and Adrian, dear. He's such a nice man! I always liked him, and now he's older—well . . .' her eyes pleaded with Chris despite Chris's closed look.

'I came down to partner him at the dinner because someone else let him down,' Chris said. 'Don't try to make anything of it, Mum.'

Mrs Hart sighed and later said to her husband, 'I don't know what's wrong with Chris. A lovely man like Adrian and she behaves as though he's just anybody!'

Alex Hart laughed. 'Ellen, you must stop romancing! Chris knows her own mind best. If she's not in love with him, she's not, and that's all there is to it.'

Ellen sighed. 'I know, but I do wish she'd meet someone nice and settle down back here.' She shrugged. 'Oh, well . . .'

Chris and Rita went to see Mrs Forster as soon as surgery was over for the day. The old lady's complexion was rather grey and she'd had several attacks in quick succession, she told them reluctantly. After a thorough examination, Chris agreed with Rita that hospitalisation was advisable in order to monitor her treatment more carefully.

Over a cup of tea Chris tried to persuade Mrs Forster to go to hospital for a few days, but the old lady was adamant. 'Once they get you in there you're lucky to get out again! Besides, who'd look after Fred and Smokey and the birds?'

Fred was the overfed dachshund and Smokey an elderly spoilt Persian cat, which Chris thought was probably not a pet that it was wise for an asthmatic to have, but she didn't dare say so. The birds were apparently the wild birds, magpies, kokkaburras and so on, that came into Mrs Forster's garden.

'I'm sure we could find someone to look after them all while you're away,' Chris said. 'It wouldn't be for long.'

Mrs Forster's lips thinned and Chris could see that nothing short of an earthquake would shift her. So she did not pursue the matter then. An unwilling patient, coerced into going into hospital, would be hard to treat. Emotional factors could often have a deleterious effect on asthma patients. It was essential that the old lady went willingly.

Chris wrote a prescription for an alternative inhalant and a linctus, and Rita promised to call daily to check on the patient.

'Perhaps if you could get her up to Outpatients,' Chris suggested as they went out to their cars, 'the staff might be able to take it from there if we warn them.'

'I'll try,' agreed Rita, 'but you saw what she's like!' She smiled rather sadly. 'It's not easy growing old on your own.'

'No, it isn't,' said Chris. 'It's not an easy problem to solve.'

The next day Chris found an opportunity to discuss the old lady with Adrian, as she was one of his father's patients. He listened sympathetically, then said, 'Hmm, it's a difficult one . . .'

'The problem might resolve itself,' said Chris. 'Sooner or later she'll probably be a critical broncho-pneumonia case.'

Her eyes met his and for a moment Mrs Forster's plight was secondary to the sharp physical response to him that ran along her nerves like heat filling the coils of a radiator. They were alone in the lounge at the Centre. It was the end of the day and they were probably the only ones still there.

He came closer, and there was something behind his smile which disturbed her.

'You're quite a hit with Dad's patients, did you know?' he said.

Chris was startled. 'They've all been very friendly.'

He looked deeply into her widening eyes. He loved that slightly startled look she had when she was being paid an unexpected compliment. It had always been her unawareness of herself, her natural modesty, that had attracted him. Even now, a mature woman, she had an air of innocence still about her, and yet professionally she was easily able to command confidence and respect. His respect for her had increased tenfold since that night in Melbourne. He had gone through agonies on her behalf, but she hadn't needed his sympathy. She'd met the situation with dignity and bravery as he supposed she would meet any situation in her life.

'Mother's always bumping into people in supermarkets and the post office, and chatting on the phone. Your reputation is growing,' he told her.

Chris coloured with embarrassment. 'Well, that's nice to know, I suppose.'

His hand caught her arm as she seemed about to go, and he turned her towards him. 'Chris . . .' His voice was soft and husky and the hunger in his eyes was clearly visible. Chris tried to step back, but both his arms folded quickly around her and drew her tightly into their circle. Her blood surged involuntarily as the warmth of his body flowed to her and he said softly against her ear, 'Chris, there's been something missing in my life all these years, and I could never pinpoint exactly what it was. I know now. It was you . . . I tried to forget you, but . . .'

'Adrian, please—you're making a big thing out of something that isn't . . .'

He was fierce suddenly and gripped her almost savagely. 'Chris, I love you! Don't you understand? I haven't stopped loving you all these years.'

'No, Adrian, you mustn't!' The words were wrenched out of her painfully.

He didn't answer but covered her mouth with his and fiercely sought his answer in her response. Chris's head whirled with crazy thoughts as her emotions flared. She didn't doubt that he would marry her regardless of the truth, but she mustn't be weak enough to let him. She must be strong enough for both of them. She must resist the urge to fling her arms around his neck and draw his head closer to hers, to take his loving lips with the fervour that would tell him what he wanted to know.

It was sheer selfishness to imagine that he could be hers to have and to hold forever. She had won that battle years ago and she mustn't show weakness now. The conflict within her became a real physical pain in the pit of her stomach and every nerve quivered with emotional agony as she pulled back from the brink of giving in to her desperate need for him.

He raised his head, threading his fingers through her hair, tracing the shape of her face with his other hand, kissing her rigid mouth with quickfire bursts and then with langourous tenderness. She suffered the onslaught rigidly, determined to discourage him.

Exasperated with her, he said hoarsely, 'Chris, what is the matter with you? Why do you fight me when I know perfectly well you don't want to?'

She regarded him frigidly and at length he let her go reluctantly, the appeal in his eyes so potent it was almost impossible to deny him any longer. But was it love he still felt for her, she thought in self-defence, or merely a reawakened physical desire?

What really did her own feelings amount to? Physical contact with a man had not been much part of her life for a long time. She avoided involvements with men as much as she could. Her body was starved for the touch of a warm, loving male, her emotions ached for the release of loving, but that wasn't necessarily love in its true sense. It was hardly surprising, she told herself, that she and Adrian were drawn to each other now. After all, they had been before. But she knew that where she was concerned, she was talking rubbish. She loved him—always had.

'It's time I went home,' she said, a catch in her voice.

He rumpled her smooth dark hair and pulled her impulsively and hard against him, holding her head against his broad chest, nuzzling her hair with his chin and encircling her waist with his other hand, pressing her slender frame so tightly against his that she almost felt her bones crack.

'Let me go, please, Adrian,' she begged, her voice muffled in his jacket.

With an impatient sigh he pushed her away. 'Go, then, go home to your cold, lonely bed and stop tormenting me!'

Chris flashed an outraged look. 'I don't torment you! You torment yourself! You're getting melodramatic, what's more!'

He laughed harshly at that. 'You're right, I do, and I am! You have that effect on me. You turned my life upside down once before and now, damn you, you're doing it again.'

'Shall I leave—leave Mount William, I mean?' Chris said, suddenly perturbed.

He reached out to her again and grasped her upper arms. 'No, please don't do that, Chris. You're doing a great job here . . .'

'Well, don't make it difficult for me,' she said, an unfamiliar hardness in her tone. It was like plunging knives into her own heart to treat him so coldly. She added quickly, 'Your father was talking about starting work again soon the last time I saw him.'

Adrian accepted the change of subject. 'He won't come back full time. We've made him promise that. Obviously he must do something, though. He can't moulder away reading medical journals and watching television. He'd go crazy.' He grinned suddenly. 'Mother and I have told him he's to be the new locum!'

Chris mustered a smile. 'Good! He can take over from me right after Christmas. I'd like to leave just before Christmas if that's all right with you, so I can spend time with my parents before I go back to Mali.'

'You've been given the OK to go back?'

'Not finally. I'll have to pass a medical first, but I've heard from Wayne Rogers, the Director of the Foundation . . .' His expression of surprise made her break off.

'Wayne Rogers!' he exclaimed. 'I wonder if he's the Wayne Rogers who was at med school with me.'

'Very likely,' Chris said. 'He's about your age and a Melbourne man.'

They talked about the Foundation for a few minutes, and finally Adrian looked hard at her and said, 'Chris, I admire your dedication, but you're not single-handedly responsible for the health of the entire developing world! You have a right to some happiness too . . .' he broke off, ashamed of his selfishness.

Chris didn't answer. She picked up her bag and said goodnight. She felt all churned up again. She had come very close in the past few minutes to telling him the truth about why there was no possible future for them together.

Adrian called to her as she left, 'Don't forget you're on emergency call this week.'

She turned briefly. 'No, I haven't forgotten. Top of the list!' He looked like a forlorn child in the shadows and her heart ached for him. Pretending she did not love him was going to take a heavy toll of her, she knew, over the next few weeks. She must not let wishful thinking weaken her.

It was the following night when she was woken from a deep sleep by the telephone ringing. Instantly she snapped into wakefulness, her subconscious knowing it was sure to be a summons to a case.

In less than ten minutes she was on her way to a patient on a farm a few kilometres out of town. A short time later she had seen the youth carefully loaded into the ambulance which she had called as soon as she had diagnosed appendicitis.

She lingered briefly for a cup of tea in the kitchen of the farmhouse with the boy's parents, reassuring them and chatting. They thanked her profusely and were apologetic about calling her out in the middle of the night.

As she set off back along the bush track to the main road, she realised that it was past one a.m. And it was raining. To the rhythmic scooping of the windscreen wipers, her mind slipped into low gear. She yawned. The adrenalin had stopped flowing and she was ready for sleep again. It wasn't until she turned on to the main road that she suddenly became aware that something had been wrong with the car for the past couple of kilometres. By the time she saw that the fuel gauge was low, the car was coughing badly. It finally came to a shuddering halt and she faced the awful realisation that she was out of petrol. In the middle of nowhere, it seemed.

She peered into the black night. If there was a moon it was hidden behind low cloud. The rain was coming down steadily. The farm she had visited was now far behind. There were no lights from any other habitation that she could see, and even if there were houses nearby they were indiscernible in the dark. People didn't leave lights burning all night for travellers who foolishly ran out of petrol.

'What a mug I am!' Chris exclaimed aloud.

She had two options. One was to walk back to town, a distance she judged would be seven or eight kilometres. Or she could spend the night in the car and hope someone would come along early in the morning. If she walked she would get drenched at once in her light jacket and with no umbrella. If she stayed, she would spend a chilly and somewhat uncomfortable night, but at least there was a rug in the car. After a few moments' consideration she opted for staying put.

'Serves me right,' she muttered, pulling the blanket around her. She had barely snuggled down under it, however, when headlights beamed along the road from the direction she had come. Chris flung off the blanket and leapt out of the car, heedless of the rain, waving her arms to flag it down. The car was weaving all over the road and, too late to change her mind about hailing it, Chris realised that the driver was probably drunk.

When it stopped and she saw who the driver was, she didn't know whether to be astonished or relieved. It was

Paul.

'Chris!' he peered at her bedraggled figure and said anxiously, 'Have I got the DTs?' He scrambled out and almost fell into her arms. She needed all her strength to support him.

'Get back in the car, Paul,' she ordered, adding accusingly, 'You've been drinking!'

He looked at her blearily, the rain running down his nose as ludicrously as it was down hers. 'I was sober when I left them but, God, I feel terrible now. I keep seeing two of you!' He added with a flash of realisation, 'What on earth are you doing out here alone at this time of night?'

'I was called to a case, and on my way home I ran out of fuel,' she said sheepishly. As he lurched again, she said, 'For God's sake, Paul, get back in the car.'

He dragged her in beside him and Chris said, 'I wasn't expecting anyone to come by so late, so I was just tucking myself up for the night. Where have you been?'

'I had dinner with some friends who go windsurfing with me,' he answered, unresentful of her curiosity. Then he looked at her with a mildly predatory look. 'What luck, being marooned alone with you on a deserted road in the middle of the night . . .'

As he reached for her, she said sternly, 'Paul!'

He pulled a wry face. 'Sorry. I was rather unwise, I fear. I must have drunk too much wine. I seem to remember someone trying to make me stay the night, but I stubbornly refused. Don't worry, Chrissie love, I'm in no state to take advantage of you—in fact I wish you'd drive me home . . . I don't feel very well . . .'

The pathetic expression on his face almost made Chris laugh. 'You look terrible!' she said unsympathetically. 'Hang on a minute and I'll be right with you.'

She collected her bag and the rug from her own car, locked it securely and ran back to Paul. He was now slumped in the passenger seat and snoring noisily. Chris drew a quick breath. He could so easily have fallen asleep over the wheel and run off the road . . . smashed into a tree. She shuddered as she threw the rug over him.

With her feet squelching in her shoes every time she pressed her foot on the brake, Chris drove back to town. As they reached the outskirts she realised that she didn't know where Paul lived. She pulled up and shook him awake.

'Paul! What's your address?'

His head lolled and he mumbled incoherently. Chris slammed a fist on the steering wheel. His address was probably in his wallet, maybe on something in the glove-box, and he must have house keys somewhere on him. But conducting a search seemed somehow a violation. She decided in the end it would be simpler to take him to her place.

He stirred sufficiently to aid her in walking him into the house, and when she propelled him into the lounge room and pushed him on to the couch, he grinned at her muzzily. He wasn't quite as wet as she was, but when she ordered him to remove his clothes he just continued to grin vacantly at her.

'All right, if you won't do it yourself . . .' she said grittily, and proceeded to strip him down to his underwear, then got him on his feet and propelled him towards the bathroom.

He became briefly aware and protested loudly, 'Chris! Really!'

'Oh, for goodness' sake, Paul, I'm a doctor!' she exploded, keeping him on his feet until she got him back to the living room again. He collapsed on the couch and she covered him with blankets and shoved a pillow under his head. He was dead to the world in seconds.

Chris peeled off her own saturated clothes and took a hot shower. She fell wearily into bed at last and plunged into a deep and dreamless sleep, not waking until the alarm shrilled at its usually early hour.

Tiptoeing out to the living room, she found a rather dishevelled but very contrite Paul sitting on the edge of the couch with his head in his hands.

He winced as she raised his head to look at her. 'What happened? How the hell did I get here? Oh, God, my head!'

Chris told him. Paul wiped his hand across his forehead. 'Is that true? I can't remember a thing. I must have had a skinful. What a lunatic I was to try and drive home.'

'It was lucky for me you did, or I'd have spent an uncomfortable night in my car.'

He grinned sheepishly. 'I reckon it was luckier for me.' A shudder passed over him. 'I could have easily wrapped myself around a tree . . . Thank goodness you stopped me before I did!'

'I'm going to make coffee,' Chris said. 'Do you want to have a shower first?'

Paul staggered to his feet. 'No, thanks all the same. I'll just swallow a coffee—black and very sweet, thanks—and get out of your way.' His face was pale and his eyes glassy. 'I've got one hell of a hangover. I guess I'd better not try to put in an appearance today.' He paused, and looked at her hopefully. 'Would it be stretching friendship too far to ask you to tone things down a bit?' He grinned faintly. 'Besides, there's no need for you to raise doubts about your reputation. I'll just phone in and say I'm ill.'

Chris pointed out, 'I have to fetch my car, and explain how I got back to town last night. I'd rather not make an intrigue of it.'

'You can say what happened if you must,' he conceded, 'but you needn't tell everyone I was drunk. Just tell them I gave you a lift. No one will know I stayed the night. I'll say I ate something and woke up bilious!'

Chris agreed. She hurried out to the kitchen and made the coffee, putting slices of bread in the toaster at the same time. Paul shortly joined her, looking very shaky.

Chris said, 'I'd better drive you . . .'

He flatly refused. 'No, I'm all right! You've done enough. I just feel a bit crook now. It's not all that far.'

Chris wasn't happy letting him drive himself, but she had no chance of winning a stand-up fight with him. She had to let him go and cross her fingers that he wouldn't do anything foolish. The streets were almost empty so early in the morning. He wasn't likely to meet much traffic.

He looked at her with, momentarily, a familiar glint in his eyes. 'Well, imagine! I spent the night at your house! And you undressed me and put me to bed!'

His eyes drifted lazily over her for a moment, admiring what he saw despite his condition. 'You look very fetching in a negligee!'

Chris said curtly, 'This is an old cotton housecoat!' She hoped he wasn't going to feel obliged to make a pass at her. 'If you're not going to take a shower, I am,' she said. 'I don't want to be late. You can let yourself out.'

'Marching orders—all right,' he said, and staggered out of the kitchen.

Chris heaved a sigh of relief when she heard his car drive off. While she was under the shower, she decided to ask Rose to drive her out to pick up her car. Rose was always at the Centre early, so there might be time to do it before surgery started.

As Chris expected, Rose was in early. As soon as Chris had explained last night's predicament, Rose offered to drive her out to fetch her car before Chris even had a chance to ask. As soon as Jill arrived, they left, stopping at a garage to pick up a can of petrol.

The car was only fifteen minutes out of town, so they were back in forty, only a few minutes behind time for the start of surgery. Meanwhile Paul had phoned. That meant a few extra patients for the rest of them. Most people, however, made appointments for another day.

Chris worked her way conscientiously through her list as usual. She did not break for coffee, but continued on until lunchtime. She was still running behind and could spare only half an hour for lunch. She was chatting to Graham when Adrian walked in. He glowered at her and she was shocked to see that he was in a very bad mood. In fact he was exceedingly angry, and it seemed it was with her, as she discovered the moment Graham left them.

'What did you do to Paul?' he demanded sarcastically.

'Do to him?' she echoed, wondering uneasily why he was asking.

'He's sick today.'

'Yes, I heard. I've been seeing some of his patients.' She added cautiously, 'He told you what happened last night?'

'I haven't spoken to him, and I doubt if he'd tell me what happened!' The scathing tone was so unlike him, Chris flinched. He went on, 'I know he spent the night at your house. What happened . . .'

Chris made an explosive sound of outrage, but he wouldn't let her speak.

'There's no point in your denying it. He was seen leaving your house at seven this morning.'

Chris felt the guilty colour flood into her cheeks although she had no reason to feel guilty. 'Who . . .?'

'Rita. She was passing and saw him come out of your front door. Looking somewhat dishevelled, she said. Presumably you were both too preoccupied all night even to hear the telephone ringing. Or did you just ignore it?' His fury seemed to be reaching explosion point. Before Chris could grapple with what he was suggesting, he went on, 'You were on call, remember? But a visit from your lover was more important than answering emergency calls. Patients don't matter when you're enjoying yourself.'

'That's a despicable thing to say! It isn't true . . .'

'Isn't it? When there was no reply from your number, they rang me since my number was next. It wasn't a serious case as it happens, but a doctor who neglects to answer her telephone when she's on call just because it's a lousy wet night and she's entertaining her lover . . .'

'How dare you!' Chris raised her voice, then realising she could be overheard, lowered it. 'It wasn't like that at all. Adrian, I can explain.'

'Look, I don't mind being called out at night,' he said, 'but when the first number on the list is too busy in bed to answer emergencies, I take a dim view of it. I don't mind taking your calls if necessary, but you can't expect other people to nurture your love life!'

'I don't—didn't!' Chris felt her voice rising to a shriek and damped it down. Gratingly, she said, 'For goodness' sake, Adrian, give me credit for a little integrity!'

'You deny he spent the night at your place?' His lips curled cynically.

'No, I don't. He did. But . . .'

'Spare me the excuses, Chris.' He turned away, but Chris could not let him go without forcing him to listen to her explanation. She grabbed his arm.

'Adrian, will you just listen for a minute . . .'

He shook her hand away and folded his arms across his chest, glaring at her. She had only once before seen him so angry, she remembered, and that had been eight years ago when she had told him it was all over between them. He'd assumed then that there must be someone else. Jealousy and anger had flared then as now. Chris swallowed hard.

Quietly she explained what had happened. Gradually his face changed, but she could see he was having difficulty accepting her story.

'Ask Paul,' she said. 'He'll tell you. Check with the Morrisons, and Rose will tell you she drove me out to fetch my car this morning. I simply wasn't at home when the second call came. I was stranded on the road. Fortunately Paul came along and gave me a lift.' There was still no need, she thought, to tell him that Paul had been drunk.

'If you'd checked your tank that wouldn't have been necessary,' he said grumpily.

'I know. I'm sorry about that. I was preoccupied . . .'

'With Paul,' he suggested, scathing again.

'Whatever the reason,' she flared, 'it's no business of yours!' She regretted the flare instantly. It only added fuel to his fury and made her look more guilty.

'So it happened as you said,' Adrian conceded, 'and he drove you home. He stayed the night. Very nice, I'm sure. And now he's sick. What's he suffering from—overwork?'

Chris almost raised her hand to strike him. 'How dare you! How dare you say that? That's vile and crude. I think you owe me an apology.'

He stubbornly refused to apologise and Chris refused to tell him that Paul had been drunk. She could hardly therefore blame him for jumping to conclusions. It sounded very lame, saying he was ill, hardly a good enough reason for staying at her house, but she had to say something.

'Paul was ill. You know how suddenly food poisoning can strike. I dosed him up and I thought I ought to keep an eye on him in case he got worse. He slept on the couch in my living room.'

'If he was so ill, why didn't you drive him straight to the hospital?' Adrian demanded.

Chris was weary of the inquisition. 'You know Paul. He refused to go, and I could hardly manhandle him.'

Adrian's scepticism was still showing. Damn you, Paul, Chris thought. And suddenly she wondered why she was bothering to defend herself. Let Adrian think there was something between her and Paul if he wanted to. Let him learn to despise her. She'd be easier for him to forget then.

She faced him defiantly. 'If you've finished castigating me and prying into my private life, I'd like to finish my lunch. I'm late already.'

Adrian withdrew a step. His face was hard, his eyes still accusing. She was beyond his understanding. All he knew was that he'd felt like wringing Paul Czernik's neck this morning when Rita had casually remarked that she'd seen Paul emerging from Chris' house looking a bit worse for wear. It was no exaggeration to say he'd seen red. He'd been going to tear a strip off Paul and then had been denied that relief because Paul was supposedly sick.

Well, maybe Chris was telling the truth, but it still rankled that Paul had stayed the night at her house. He'd been racked with jealousy at the thought of them together, but he couldn't stop her seeing Paul. If she wanted to have a casual affair with his partner that was their business. He could only stand by and feel shredded inside because she didn't love him. And yet he'd felt so strongly . . . that she just might still . . .

He looked at her now, coolly and calmly eating her sandwiches, and he wanted to pick her up bodily and crush her to him and never let another man touch her. But he could do that if she wanted him to, and she was making it very clear that she didn't want him to . . .

He went over to the urn and squirted coffee savagely into a cup. He glanced at her. 'Coffee?' he offered brusquely.

'Yes, thank you.' She needed liquid to force the sandwiches down.

He placed hers in front of her, then said gruffly, 'I'm sorry I spoke roughly to you. Obviously you couldn't have answered that second call if you were already out. What else you did last night is your own business. I apologise for suggesting it was also mine.'

Chris met his eyes bravely. How she wanted to rush into his arms! 'That's all right,' she said. 'I'm sorry you were called out too. If I hadn't broken down I would probably have been back in time to take the call. I'll be careful not to run low on petrol again.'

Adrian sank into a chair and gulped the scalding coffee.

'Aren't you eating?' she asked conversationally, as though their row had never erupted.

'No.'

'Have a sandwich. I've got too much.' The truth was she wasn't hungry. 'You ought to have something. All that neat caffeine will rot your stomach lining!'

A ghost of a smile flickered across his lips. Chris's heart ached intolerably for him, her arms ached to wind themselves around him. She chewed her sandwich. It was like trying to eat cardboard. She offered the plate and he took one, squeezing it in his fingers without eating it.

'You'll make it very indigestible doing that,' she said, and he looked across at her and without speaking opened his mouth and crammed the whole triangle in. Shredded lettuce and a globule of tomato juice lingered on his chin. He wiped his mouth casually with the back of his hand.

'Thanks,' he said.

Chris glanced at the clock. 'I'd better be going.'

As she was leaving the room, he said, 'You're coming for dinner tonight, I believe.'

Chris had temporarily forgotten Janet Gilmore's invitation. 'Yes,' she said, and wished she didn't have to go.

'Don't let my bad temper put you off,' he said, offering a kind of olive branch. 'Mother and Dad are still reasonable company.'

Chris felt tears welling up in his eyes and desperately didn't want him to see them, so she kept her head averted. 'About seven-thirty?'

'Yes, that'll be fine,' Adrian said. 'See you then.'

# CHAPTER NINE

CHRIS did not see Adrian again until the evening. He had gone up to the hospital, Rose told her, when the last patients had gone and they were preparing to leave themselves.

It had been a busy afternoon. Paul's absence had caused only a minor traffic jam of patients, but it had seemed to be a day when every consultation needed longer time than usual. Usually some brief consultations, some lengthier ones, tended to balance out the allotted appointment times so that the day's work was fitted reasonably comfortably into the hours available. Tonight it was after seven, however.

'And I thought we were going to finish early today,' moaned Carole, leaving Chris and Rose to walk together to the car-park.

'You'll be glad of an early night, Chris,' Rose said with a smile, 'after last night's adventure.' They paused by her car.

Her confrontation with Adrian at lunchtime had drained Chris far more than the events of the previous night, but she couldn't tell Rose that. 'I'm having dinner with the Gilmores,' she said, 'but I daresay I'll be able to get away early.'

Rose gave her a studied look. 'I think Janet would like you as a daughter-in-law.'

Chris was so taken aback at the remark, she blushed. 'Do you? Oh, no, I don't think so. She knows I'm going back to Africa soon. The fact that Adrian and I knew each other years ago doesn't mean anything.' She hadn't expected Rose to be so perceptive.

'No, of course not,' said Rose quickly. She slid her key in the car door and smiled. 'It would be nice, though, if it did. Adrian needs a wife . . .' She broke off and went on apologetically. 'None of my business! Sorry!'

Chris managed a light retort. 'Oh, I'm used to people trying to matchmake.'

Rose got into her car but did not close the door. She said, 'So you're not keen on Paul either?'

'Heavens, no!' Her laugh now was more genuine.

'Good,' said Rose seriously. 'He's definitely not your type.' She looked Chris over quizzically. 'Adrian is, though, and I sometimes think . . .' Again she broke off. 'There I go again, busybodying! Have a nice evening, and don't get into any scrapes!'

Chris was a couple of minutes behind her leaving the car-park, and as she drove away, preoccupied as she always seemed to be these days with thoughts of Adrian, she noticed a blue utility pull away from the kerb behind her, but attached no significance to the fact that it seemed fleetingly familiar.

She was still worrying about whether the atmosphere would be strained this evening as a result of her row with Adrian at lunchtime, when she parked in the driveway of her house, leaving the car there as she would be needing it later. As she got out she noticed out of the corner of her eye the blue utility cruising past. She was putting her key in the front door when she heard a squeal of brakes and turned at the sound. The blue ute had come back and was now parked outside her gate. Chris started first in perplexity, then with apprehension as a youth got out, vaulted the gate and loped down the path to the creeper-shrouded verandah.

'What. . .? Who . . .?' She instinctively tried to open the door and escape from him because she sensed danger, but she wasn't quick enough. Her wrist was grasped in a vice and a clammy hand was clamped over her mouth. She knew now why the utility had seemed vaguely familiar, but she did not know the youth. It was not the driver who had knocked John Portman off his bicycle, but the vehicle was the same one. This youth was taller and very strong. He pushed her roughly through the open door and kicked it shut behind him. Chris struggled ineffectually as he rammed her against the wall.

Oh, my God, what am I going to do? Her brain was reeling and she was angry as well as terrified. How dared he! Nothing like this had ever happened before. She'd had some bad moments with drunks in Casualty, and in Mali there had been occasional problems; once a burglar had forced an entry into her bungalow, but he had not harmed her; she sensed that burglary was not this intruder's purpose.

His face leered in the gloom close to hers. 'Scared stiff, aren't you?' he said hastily. 'Good. You'd better be. You're wondering what I'm going to do to you, aren't you? Well—nothing right now, Doctor, but if you don't think again about the evidence you're going to give against my mate . . .'

Chris tried valiantly to bite the hand that covered her mouth even though she knew she would probably incur worse punishment. She was trembling from fury and fright and she was reacting more from instinct than reason.

'Quite a little wildcat, aren't you?' he said, releasing her.

She would have made a dash to escape him if she hadn't been brought up hard against the glint of steel in his fist. He stifled her scream with his hand slapped hard again across her mouth. His features were scarcely discernible in the gloomy hallway, but she sensed that it would be unwise to antagonise him further.

He laid the flat edge of the steel blade against her cheek. 'I wouldn't want to spoil a pretty face,' he said menacingly. 'So don't you be so sure in court that Ralph was the guy you saw that day. Because if you are, I'll be back . . .' His voice was loaded with menace, but he broke off at the sound of a car door slamming. It sounded close. A moment later, there was the sound of footsteps on the path and the verandah. Then the doorbell rang.

Caught off guard for a moment, the intruder took his hand from Chris's mouth and instantaneously she let out a very healthy scream. He panicked and ran out through the back of the house. As the sound of breaking glass came from the rear, the front door burst open.

'Christ!' Adrian stood poised in the doorway for one incredulous second. 'What in heavens name . . .?'

'Out the back,' Chris croaked. 'He's gone out the back way . . .' She gazed at Adrian with thankfulness and bewilderment. He was the last person she had expected to see. 'No, don't go after him, he's got a knife . . .' She caught hold of him desperately. 'He'll have got away.'

He clasped her trembling body in his arms. 'Are you all right?'

'Yes—I think so . . .' Chris whispered. 'The blue ute . . .'

Adrian left her and dashed back through the front door, but the ute was already speeding away. Adrian did not give chase as he knew he would probably lose the offender. He was too concerned about Chris anyway. She had crumpled into a heap on the floor and was sobbing.

He sank to his knees and gathered her into his arms and carried her into the living room. At least she seemed unhurt. He had arrived in the nick of time, he felt sure. She clung to him and he held her on his lap, soothing her as though she were a small child.

Eventually the shaking subsided and she gulped and whispered, 'Oh, Adrian, it was horrible!'

'It's all right now, love—he's gone. Did he hurt you?'

'No. He just scared me half to death. Oh, God, it was awful! I thought he was going to . . .' She began shaking again. 'I didn't know what he was going to do.'

'I'll get you something to calm you,' he said, shifting her on to the couch beside him.

'No—it's all right, Adrian,' Chris insisted. 'I'll be OK in a minute.' She moistened her lips. 'Just a glass of water will do.'

He fetched it quickly and held it to her lips because her hands were still shaking too much to hold the glass steady. He sat beside her, a bulwark of strength and comfort, and gradually she ceased to tremble.

'Was he in the house when you came in?' Adrian asked.

Chris shook her head and told him what had happened. 'He must have watched me leave the Centre and followed me home. I saw the ute behind me, but it didn't register. It wasn't the hit-and-run driver, it was one of his mates, so he said. The idea was to frighten me into not being so certain about indentification at the trial. I didn't have a chance to tell him I wouldn't even be there, that I've already given my evidence in an affidavit. He threatened me with a knife and said he'd get me if I didn't do as he said.' She buried her face against Adrian's chest. It was as though their argument earlier in the day had never happened. 'I was petrified! Thank goodness you came . . .' She looked up at him. 'Why did you?'

He cradled her head against him. 'I felt pretty rotten about tearing a strip off you earlier today. I had no right to. So I came to collect you, to give me a chance to apologise to you properly. I scarcely even noticed the ute parked outside. I was surprised to find you'd left your keys in the door and I was ready to chide you for it. When you screamed . . .' He pulled her tighter against him and his warmth and protectiveness enfolding her made her heart race for a different reason. 'If your keys hadn't been in the door I'd have smashed it down. You're sure he didn't hurt you?'

'No. And I don't think he would have done. Not this time. He just came to threaten me.'

'The police will get him too, I hope. If he was driving his mate's ute, it probably won't be too difficult. They're a couple of thugs, obviously.' He tilted her chin. 'Chris, if he'd harmed you, I'd . . .!'

Chris had no resistance to offer when he kissed her this time. She clung to him with all the deep-rooted need that her fear had unleashed and she responded with her soul to the tenderness and soothing quality of his embrace. It didn't matter that she had vowed never to let herself be trapped in this situation again. She was not in control of her emotions now. They were far stronger than she was and in the next few minutes she unwittingly convinced Adrian that she was not as indifferent to him as she tried to pretend.

But he said nothing as they drew apart. If this was the beginning of something—a whole new beginning perhaps, which he hardly dared contemplate—he would have to tread very carefully in order not to spoil it. Love was such a fragile thing, and could be so easily fragmented. Chris, in fear and relief, had turned to him wholeheartedly, but later she might regret her weakness and try to build up her defences again. Somehow he would prevent that. He would convince her that they belonged together. Adrian smiled confidently as he held her tightly in his arms.

'I'd better warn Mother we'll be a bit late,' he said at last. 'And I'd better do something about the glass pane in your back door.'

Chris still lay with her head resting against his chest. She felt that she never wanted to move away from him, but she stirred and said anxiously, 'Yes, your mother will be wondering what's happened to us.'

Adrian smiled into her pale face and smoothed the dark tendrils of hair clinging to her forehead away. He wished he could smooth away as easily the lingering fear in her grey eyes. He said, 'Doctors' wives and mothers never wonder—they know! She'll guess something has come up. But I'll ring her and tell her we'll be there as soon as we can. We'll have to report to the police first.'

'Adrian, do we have to?' Chris asked, dreading it.

He gripped her shoulders. 'Yes, we must. And they'd better get their hands on that thug pretty smartly too!' His grim expression became gentle as he looked at her. 'You shouldn't be living alone.'

Chris eased away from him. 'Adrian, please don't blow this up out of proportion. I'm perfectly all right living alone. I've been doing it for years. He won't try anything like that again, I'm sure.'

He looked doubtful and said, 'Well, at least stay with us tonight.' As Chris stood up, he reached for her hands and held them tightly.

Looking down at him, she realised that in the past few minutes she had betrayed her feelings completely. She had undone everything she had tried to do to convince him that she no longer had any feelings for him. She withdrew her hands slowly and turned away. A surge of love overwhelmed her and again she thought maybe it could work after all—how easily that treacherous thought sneaked in! The temptation to tell him the truth then was strong, but she hesitated. It required a time that was less emotional, with time to discuss it rationally. She needed to resolve the conflict within herself first. The past half hour had convinced her, if she'd needed any convincing, that Adrian was still the only man she wanted to give her life, her love, her all to. Leaving him again was going to tear her apart. But dared she believe in a future with him—could she ask him to make the sacrifice he would have to make in order to marry her?

'I'd better get cleaned up,' she said. 'You phone your mother. I won't be long.'

'I'll see what I can do about the door,' Adrian said, despite her protests that they could lock the laundry door into the house until tomorrow. 'Tomorrow I'll get you a glazier,' he said.

She smiled. 'I'm quite capable of organising things like that myself!'

He hugged her tightly. She was joking again. She was all right. 'I know. But wouldn't you like to feel pampered for once?'

She giggled. 'I'm a feminist, Adrian!'

He looked with mock severity into her face. 'Sure! And I'm a masculinist! Go and wash your face and I'll board up your window.'

Making a deliberate effort to calm her shattered nerves, Chris slid quickly under the shower. The massaging water made her feel much better. After being manhandled and terrorised by the youth she felt the need to be thoroughly cleansed of the whole horrible incident, and the steaming needle-sharp jets of water from the shower were a symbolic balm to her nerves.

As she was dressing, she heard the sound of hammering and smiled to herself. Adrian was nothing if not practical! She closed her eyes for a moment and felt his arms around her comforting her, his lips on hers passionate as well as soothing, and the thought of having his love and protection for the rest of her life was almost too strong to be denied. But I must keep things in perspective, she told herself firmly.

Chris did not want to stay the night at the Gilmores'. She was perfectly certain she would be quite safe at home and that she would not be bothered again, but she didn't want to seem ungrateful or too abrasively independent, so she shoved a few things into a holdall and was ready to go when Adrian had finished his task.

He had found tools and a sheet of hardboard in the garage, luckily. Her back door was now firmly secured.

'That should do it!' he said with satisfaction at his handiwork, as she walked in, and he turned to look at her.

She had changed into black velvet trousers and a crushed strawberry skivvy, topped by a multi-coloured embroidered jacket. Adrian wanted to envelop her in his arms again, but he resisted the urge. He felt he was on firmer ground for the first time since he'd met her again, and he was afraid to do anything that might bring back the quicksands.

'Thank you—that looks very solid,' Chris said. 'You're quite a handyman.'

'I have my talents,' he agreed with a smirk, and they both laughed. The rapport between them had never been better, he thought. It was just like the old days before she'd suddenly thrown him over.

'What did your mother say?' Chris asked. She was pale and there was a lingering terror in her eyes, but she had recovered her composure and her hands were no longer shaking. She looked very fragile, very beautiful, he thought, and so vulnerable. Yet in many way, she was tough. She had to be, he knew, to work where she did. He felt a new surge of love and protectiveness towards her.

'She just groaned when I said we'd be late because something had come up.' Adrian said. 'I said we'd explain when we got there. I didn't want to alarm her unduly.' He let his gaze drift admiringly over Chris. 'You look lovely, Chris. No one would guess you'd just had a ghastly experience. You're very resilient.'

She pretended nonchalance. 'Oh, it takes more than the threat of violence to throw me completely!' She laughed at her own bravado.

He rested his hands on her shoulders. 'You're a plucky kid!'

'Not so much of the "Kid" if you don't mind! I'm over thirty!'

He bent and brushed his lips across hers. 'But by no means over the hill—if you hurry!'

Chris dodged away, pretending outrage now. 'That's the sort of remark smart Alecs like you, Gilmore, get severely punished for!' Her eyes were dancing. It was the sort of nonsense they'd always shared. The loving insults, she'd often called it to herself in memory. She added guilelessly, 'I've been meaning to ask you—when are you planning to retire? You must be near pension age.'

He loomed above her and caught her face between his two hands. 'For that remark, Dr Hart, I prescribe another dose of medicine!' And he kissed her lingeringly until every inch of her tingled with sensations she had long learned to do without. Adrian raised his head at last and kissed her eyes, the tip of her nose and her chin. He nuzzled his mouth into the warm hollows of her neck. 'I think we're beginning to understand one another again,' he whispered huskily.

Chris swallowed hard. She was afraid to catch hold of the happiness Adrian promised. Did she have any right to it? That Adrian could satisfy all her emotional needs, she had no doubt, but could she satisfy his? He was loving her without knowing all the facts. She must decide whether to tell him the truth, or whether to reject him again without doing so. But now was not the time. She was still shocked, and confused.

Drawing reluctantly away, Adrian said, 'We'd better go. Have you got your toothbrush?'

'Yes.' Suddenly she wished she could spend the evening here alone with him instead of going to his parents, and was irritated with herself for the thought.

Janet assured Chris when they arrived that the dinner had not spoiled and would indeed have benefited from maturing. 'Now tell us what happened,' she demanded, as Adrian poured stiff brandies for them both. 'I could tell from Adrian's tone that it was something quite unpleasant.'

Taking a deep breath, Chris explained. Recounting it made her start to tremble again, and Adrian took over, telling his parents what had happened on his arrival. Janet's gasps showed how shocked and concerned she was.

'Just as well you went to fetch her, Adrian,' she said. 'Oh, Chris, my dear, what a ghastly experience! Supposing Adrian hadn't come—it doesn't bear thinking about . . .'

Chris glanced at him thankfully. 'It was timely, yes, but I don't really think that boy would have harmed me—not this time. I was mighty relieved to see Adrian, though.'

Andrew said, 'I hope you got a good look at the ruffian, Adrian.'

'Only a glimpse as he was driving off, but I'm pretty sure I'd know him again. We both gave a full description to the police. They reckon they know him.' He added, 'I insisted that Chris spent the night here, Mother.'

'Yes, Chris, of course you must stay with us,' Janet said. She frowned anxiously. 'You ought not to be living in that house alone. It's not safe.'

'I'm all right,' Chris insisted. 'I'm very careful, Janet.

I always lock up securely at night and when I go out.' She shrugged it off. 'One has to take a few risks in life. I take plenty out in Mali, I can assure you.'

But they were all still concerned for her. She was such a slip of a girl and yet all three knew that it would be ridiculous to treat her like a vulnerable child. She was a mature young woman a capable doctor and she had an independent spirit. The only way to look after her, Adrian thought, was to marry her. And this time he was not going to be prevented from doing it, not without one hell of a fight anyway. He'd let her go too easily last time.

'I suppose all that drama has blunted your appetites,' Janet said. 'But I'd better dish up. I know you told us not to wait, Adrian, but we did.'

Chris was feeling more relaxed now and gradually the terror was receding to the back of her mind. A couple of glasses of one of Adrian's own wines helped to ease the strain her nerves had been through. It wasn't difficult to feel at ease with the Gilmores and she was grateful for their company for the evening and their invitation to stay the night.

It was still quite early when Janet kindly suggested she might feel ready for bed and took her along to the guest room. Chris was only too willing to retire. She was feeling exhausted mentally and physically, and after all the emotional upheavals of the day, she wanted to avoid being left alone with Adrian.

Next day Adrian agreed to say nothing at the clinic about Chris's experience the previous evening. She did not want a fuss made over it, she insisted, and from the point of view of repercussions from any other mates of the hit-and-run driver, it might be better to keep quiet about the incident. Janet and Andrew tried to persuade her to stay with them for a few days, but Chris would not be persuaded.

'And there's no need for you to camp on my doorsetp,' she told Adrian, when he tried to remonstrate with her. 'I'll be all right.'

Later that day he came to tell her that the police had picked up the youth who had assaulted her and he had admitted the offence. They had also charged him with several breaking and entering offences.

'He's got a long history of petty convictions, like his mate,' Adrian told her. 'There's every likelihood he'll be remanded in custody.' He added, 'And before I forget—I've arranged for a glazier to fix your door pane.'

Chris thanked him for that. She felt relieved about the intruder too. She wasn't nervous, but for a while she did take extra care that she was not being followed when she left the clinic to go home, and she was meticulous about bolting doors and windows at night as a precaution.

On Saturday, as they were preparing to leave the Centre, Adrian walked across to her as she was getting into her car.

'Doing anything tomorrow?'

'No, nothing in particular. Chores, I expect!'

'What about a trip out to my vineyard?'

Chris hesitated. She had almost decided during the past couple of days that it would be best if she kept silent about her reasons for not renewing their relationship. Always when she was almost tempted into it, her conscience would prevent her. To accept Adrian's love would be selfish. But it was hard to be indifferent to him as she knew she must, and it was even harder to be unfriendly.

'Well . . .' she said hesitantly, searching for an excuse.

'You went sightseeing with Paul,' he reminded her. 'Why not with me?'

'Do you and Paul have fair shares in everything?' she said lightly.

He caught her chin between finger and thumb. 'Depends what we're talking about. There are some things I'm not prepared to share with Paul.' And you're one of them, he thought fiercely.

Chris wriggled out of his grasp. 'Don't be so possessive!'

'Chris . . .' There was a pleading note in his voice. 'Don't tease . . .'

She wanted to go out with him. She wanted to be with him. But the closer she allowed their relationship to become, the harder it would be to walk away from him in only a few weeks' time. She battled for a moment with her conscience, and her weak will won.

'Shall I bring a picnic lunch?' she asked, taking the path with no return.

He relaxed. 'Why not? According to the forecast it's going to be fine and warm.'

Chris drove home knowing she was a fool and yet anticipating with a rare kind of joy the outing next day.

# CHAPTER TEN

As THE Weather Bureau had promised, Sunday dawned bright and sunny with no wind, but Chris dressed warmly in top clothes she could discard if she became too warm as there was still a sharpness in the early morning air. She wore green cords, a checked cotton shirt, a lightweight sweater and a zip-up anorak. That, she thought, should take care of any changes in the weather or temperature. She was up early and ready with a packed lunch by the time Adrian arrived.

He said, 'I thought I might take you sightseeing before we go to Ravensbush. You've already been to Hall's Gap, so I thought a run to Great Western and a tour of the champagne cellars. How does that sound?'

'Sounds great,' said Chris. 'Especially if we get to taste the champagne!'

'We certainly do!'

They arrived at the Seppelt champagne cellars just in time to join a tour of the underground drives where thousands of bottles of champagne and other wines were stored. It was a little eerie down in the cool dimly lit corridors which had been carved out of the granite by early pioneers in the wine industry.

'It's like a catacomb,' Chris whispered to Adrian as they followed the guide from one long passageway to another. 'You could get lost down here if you missed a turning.'

'I could think of worse fates than being lost with you and a million bottles of champagne!' said Adrian with a teasing smile, and tightened his arm around her shoulders. A tourist near them heard and flashed them an indulgent smile.

'Shh . . .' muttered Chris, embarrassed. 'Listen to what the guide's saying.'

146

Chris was facinated by the history of the cellars and the wine-growing area, and wondered why she'd never got around to visiting the district before.

Vines had been first planted in Great Western, they were told, in 1863, by two families who had come from the wine-growing area of France. The granity soil resembled that in their home country and so they were convinced they would be successful.

'They certainly were,' said Adrian.

Emerging from the underground drives at last, they entered the Shaft House, named for the original shaft from which the labyrinth of tunnels had been excavated by unemployed miners last century. In the Shaft House they were invited to sample various vintages of champagne and other sparkling wines.

'Your wines are just as good!' said Chris charitably, with a teasing grin at Adrian.

'Kind of you to say so, ma'am,' he replied drily.

'When are you going to start making champagne too?' Chris asked.

'Don't suggest it in front of Robert!' Adrian laughed. 'He's always talking about it!' He glanced at his watch. 'Come on, let's find a nice quiet spot for lunch.' He tucked their purchases under his arm and they went back to the car.

A short time later Chris was unpacking the picnic basket on a grassy bank by a creek and Adrian was deftly removing the wire from the bottle of champagne they had bought.

'This is utterly peaceful, I could stay for ever,' Chris murmured presently, lying back, with a feeling of dangerous contentment stealing over her.

Adrian moved closer. His fingers slid caressingly along her arm as he raised himself on one elbow and smiled into her eyes. 'You could . . .' he murmured, and when she didn't answer, he said, 'It's just like old times, isn't it?'

Chris let the memories wash over her. If only it could be . . . She closed her eyes because it was painful looking into Adrian's, and a moment later she felt his lips brush

hers and his body lean heavily against her. The
temptation to turn into his arms as she knew he wanted
her to was strong. It was what she wanted too, to just
relax in his arms, kiss and hold and belong with him, just
as she had before. But instead she rolled away, sat up and
brushed herself down, and not looking at him, said
briskly,

'Hadn't we better go? You said you were taking me to
see your vineyard.'

She could feel his chagrin even before she heard his
involuntary sigh, and she knew his eyes would be
perplexed and disappointed if she dared to look. She
stood up and began to repack the picnic basket.

Adrian got up too. She was so difficult to understand.
One minute he felt he had her in the palm of his hand, the
next she was as elusive as a butterfly.

'What made you buy a vineyard?' Chris asked, as they
headed towards the hills again.

'I've always had an interest in wine and viticulture. I
don't know why,' Adrian told her. 'So when I was
looking for a retreat, somewhere I could go and relax
completely, I saw Ravensbush and bought it. Mother and
Dad go there quite often too, and the rest of the family
use it as a holiday home from time to time. It's in a
pleasant spot, and since I hate being idle I can also
indulge my interest in grapes when I'm relaxing.'

'Andrew told me you have a manager who's also your
winemaker.'

'Robert Cameron. He's a wizard winemaker. He was
with one of the big companies a few years back, but he
had a coronary when he was only thirty-eight. He decided
to take it easy and he can experiment to his heart's
content on my place without the stresses of commercial
wine production. He takes immense pride in producing a
small quantity of quality wine. We've won quite a few
awards at shows.'

'Yes, your father told me,' Chris said.

'The place is empty at the moment,' Adrian went on,
'but come the school holidays, it'll be overrun with nieces

and nephews. Faye—she's Robert's wife—gathers them all under her wing along with her own three and everyone has a whale of a time. Faye's quite a bit younger than Robert and they have three under school-age children.' He glanced at her. 'You get on well with kids, don't you?'

'Usually,' she acknowledged. 'We're only three in my family, but I'm the oldest, so I had some practice. And I see plenty of children in Mali.'

'That must be one of the hard parts,' Adrian said reflectively, 'seeing children malnourished and hopeless, knowing you can't do much to help them.'

'Sometimes that's the case,' she agreed, 'but there are some very positive things happening. The people in Mali have a wonderful spirit and they're trying hard to improve things themselves, as are people all over Africa.'

They were silent for a few minutes and Chris gazed thoughtfully at the scenery flashing past, thinking that very soon it would be giving way to Mali bush again. It was some minutes before she was aware they were driving between long rows of vines.

'Is this your vineyard?' she asked, jerking back to reality.

'I was wondering when you'd notice. You were miles away, weren't you?' Adrian was smiling at her. 'Yes, this is Ravensbush. What you're seeing is mainly Hermitage and some Pinot. Robert will tell you which grapes are used to make which wine. See that screen of trees ahead, it hides the house.'

A few moments later Adrian pulled up outside an old mudbrick homestead with verandahs, chimneys and an overgrown garden. Surrounding the house were towering gum trees.

'It looks historic,' Chris commented.

'Part of it's pretty old,' Adrian told her. 'I've had it restored as faithfully as possible to the original, and the extension is in the same style, but with all modern conveniences.'

'I love it!' exclaimed Chris as she got out of the car.

She walked up to the front verandah. 'I've always wanted to live in a house like this . . .' She stopped, regretting that she had let her tongue run away with her.

Adrian was close beside her. He grasped her shoulders and turned her to him, looking searchingly into her face. 'You could if you wanted to . . .' It was the second time that day. He brushed his mouth lightly across hers and her heart speeded up at the sensations his touch evoked. She moved away, disturbed again.

'Is it haunted?' she asked, trying for a light touch to defuse the moment of being so acutely aware of each other it was like tinder about to ignite.

Adrian chuckled. 'Probably. There are a lot of strange noises at night, but that's probably only possums.' He held her arm. 'Come along in. We'll have a cup of tea.'

He showed her through the house and Chris was enchanted with it. It was hard to guess where the original house ended and the additions began, it had been integrated so cleverly.

'Your mod cons are lovely,' Chris enthused, running her fingers along the polished pine benches and worktops in the new kitchen. 'And the pot-bellied stove is perfect in the family room.'

Adrian said, 'Mother's idea.'

Chris was thinking wistfully—'family room', the place where the family ate meals, watched telvision, where the children played . . . She wandered across to gaze out of the window while Adrian filled the kettle. All at once she felt bitter at the cruel blow fate had dealt her.

As she turned, Adrian waved to someone he could evidently see through the kitchen window. A moment later the back door rattled and a woman's voice called out, 'Yoo-hoo!'

'Come in, Faye,' Adrian called.

A woman about Chris's age, with long fair hair in a ponytail, came in bearing a plate covered in cling-wrap.

'I saw you arrive,' she said, smiling at each in turn, 'so I brought you something to go with your cuppa. I baked this morning.' She uncovered the plate of reveal fresh scones and biscuits.

'Faye, this is Dr Hart—Chris,' said Adrian. 'Faye Cameron, Chris.'

'Nice to meet you, Chris,' Faye said, her shrewd blue eyes summing up, and then switching a speculative glance at Adrian. 'Will you have time to see Robert today? He wants to talk to you about some new grape variety he plans to plant.'

'We'll come over presently,' Adrian promised.

Faye left them and Adrian made the tea. 'Faye's a teacher,' he told Chris, 'and she also illustrates children's books. Mainly wildlife.'

Chris nibbled a biscuit. 'She's also a good cook. These used to be my faviourite,' she confessed sheepishly. 'Garibaldis, aren't they? We used to call them squashed-fly biscuits!'

Adrian laughed. 'So did we! I'd forgotten.' Their eyes locked for a moment, until Chris reached for another biscuit and averted hers.

He said, 'If you're cold I'll light the stove.'

'No, I'm finc,' Chris said, scttling on thc family room couch.

'I'll leave it till later, then,' Adrian said, and when Chris raised her eyebrows in a query and said, 'Later?' he announced calmly, 'I thought we'd have dinner here tonight. I'm quite a good cook myself.'

Chris was taken aback. 'Oh—I didn't realise . . .'

'We don't often have any time alone,' he said, and she was again afraid to look into his eyes.

It was so companionable sitting there drinking tea with him. They were companionable, there was no doubt about that. And this was going to be a day she would always remember, she suddenly felt strongly, a day to nurture in her heart.

Presently they walked down the track to the Camerons' house, and as they approached, they were mobbed by three small children and two dogs. Adrian scooped up the smallest child and set him astride his shoulders. The other two clung to his hands and Chris thought how easily he got along with children. He was a natural father. He introduced her to the children and they all said hello shyly and regarded her curiously.

Robert Cameron came out to meet them. He was a dark thickset man with a gypsy complexion and flashing eyes. While Adrian and Robert were talking about the new vines, Chris asked Faye about her painting and was shown her workroom and the illustrations she was working on for a book about Australian native birds.

'They're superb!' exclaimed Chris, enchanted by the exquisite detail in the watercolours. 'They almost fly off the page!'

Faye smiled modestly. 'Robert says I'll ruin my eyes.'

'Are they drawn from life?'

'Some of them. We have a lot of birds around here. They know I'm a sucker and will feed them. Did you see Nev?'

'Who's Nev?' Chris asked.

Faye grinned. 'Ask Adrian to introduce you! It's a wonder the old cadger wasn't around when you arrived. He'll be along for his supper shortly.'

Chris was intrigued, and presently, as they were walking back to the homestead, she asked Adrian about 'Nev'.

'Does he work for you?'

Adrian laughed loudly, then whistled.

'Faye wouldn't tell me,' Chris said, intrigued. 'She laughed too and said to ask you.'

Adrian grinned at her. 'When I bought this property it was called Buttercup Downs, would you believe?'

Chris pulled a face.

'My sentiments exactly. And Nev is the reason I changed it to Ravensbush.' He uttered another peiercing whistle, and suddenly a large black glossy bird appeared, half leaping, half flying along the track. He stopped and regarded them with intelligent bluish-white eyes, and said, 'Aaark!'

'A crow!' exclaimed Chris, who had never seen one so close up before. 'Isn't it big! Is it tame?'

'Nev is not an "it", if you don't mind,' reproached Adrian. 'Nev is either a he or a she, we aren't certain which, so we plumped for masculine. And please don't refer to him as a crow. Nev is an Australian Raven.'

As though to confirm it the raven made a low grating sound like a cross between a croak and a rusty hinge and the hackles under his chin rose.

'I didn't know we had ravens in Australia,' Chris said. 'He's not like the ones I've seen at the Tower of London. They're bigger.'

'Different species,' said Adrian, 'but they're all members of the corvidae family. Nev has a cousin called the Little Raven who looks very simliar but has a different call and not such prominent hackles under his chin. There's an Australian crow too, but here we see mostly ravens.'

Nev regarded them with interest. Adrian went on, 'Unfortunately, he'll never be able to fly properly. He was here when I first inspected the property. The place was derelict then. I managed to catch him and I tried to mend the wing by pinning it, but it didn't work. I had to amputate a piece of it. He can fly to low branches but he can't go very far afield. He doesn't seem to want to now. Faye feeds him and he's more or less boss of the place. He's even got her chooks bluffed. Of course when I adopted him, I had to change the name of the property to Ravensbush.'

Chris chuckled. How typical of Adrian it was! 'How was the wing damaged?' she asked.

'He was probably shot. Ravens—or crows as most people call them—aren't very popular with farmers. They're accused of killing lambs, but they don't deserve that reputation. There's scientific evidence to refute that claim, but because they eat carrion, if they're seen near a carcase they're assumed to have killed it.'

'It sounds like some medical old wives' tales,' commented Chris. 'People still persist in believing them even when science had proved they're rubbish.' She stopped and exclaimed with a laugh, 'I've just got it!

*Nev—nevermore*—you called him that after the Edgar Allan Poe poem.' She dropped her voice to a deep tone. ' *"Quoth the raven, nevermore!"* ' She laughed again. 'I used to love reciting that. It has such a spine-chilling sepulchral sound. *"Once upon a midnight dreary . . ."* '

' *". . . while I pondered weak and weary."* ' Adrian tucked her arm through his as they recited a couple of verses together and then laughingly had to stop because they couldn't remember any more.

'Perhaps it would have been kinder to put Nev down as he can't fly,' Adrian said, 'but when he looked at me with those intelligent and saucy eyes, I just couldn't. I was going to call him Grip, but Nev sounded more authentically Australian.'

Chris frowned, thinking, then nodded. 'Got it again! *Barnaby Rudge*—Dickens, of course, I'd forgotten. Barnaby's pet raven.' She added, 'At least he's free, Adrian. And he seems to be managing well enough, even if it's not as good as being able to fly. What I can't bear to see is a bird in a cage.'

'Something I've always hated too,' agreed Adrian, and they mingled smiles.

'Down to Faye's, Nev,' said Adrian. 'Suppertime!'

'Does he ever peck anyone?' Chris asked, impressed by the strong sharp beak of the raven.

'He pecked the ankles of a farm-machinery salesman once, but I think that was because he fancied his coloured socks!'

They continued on to the homestead and the raven waddled off and fluttered on to a low branch of a tree. Chris let her arm remain through Adrian's, unwilling to spoil the happiness of these precious moments when they were so at one with one another.

While he prepared what he said would be the best vegetable curry and rice she was ever likely to taste, Chris set the table and poured pre-dinner drinks as instructed. Sitting on a stool at the kitchen divider, she watched with interest Adrian's deftness in the kitchen. Once he turned and caught her smiling.

'What's so amusing?'

'You! You're so housewifely! Some men wouldn't be seen dead in the kitchen, even today. You're so competent too!'

'As you are at doctoring,' he responded cheerfully. 'There was a time when women doctors were a rarity. Times have changed, my dear, in the operating room and the kitchen!'

'I hate to mention it, but I suppose there are similarities of expertise,' she said with a grimace.

'Only if you're a carnivore,' Adrian said, and they both pulled faces.

'Sick joke!' Chris reproved.

He leaned across the counter and kissed the tip of her nose. 'You know, you're fast turning me into a vegetarian too.'

'Good. Compassion suits you. You are compassionate at heart. And not just with people. Look at the way you treated that raven.'

He regarded her for a moment as though he was about to say something, but the timer on the stove pinged and distracted him.

Half an hour later, Chris was saying sincerely, 'That *was* the best curry I ever tasted,' as she swallowed her last mouthful.

'More?'

'I shouldn't . . .'

'It isn't fattening. Not that that matters with you, you're as slim as a reed.'

'I'm not all that skinny,' she objected. 'I'm just small build.'

'But well made,' he said, his eyes teasing her. 'All the curves in the right places!'

Chris accepted a second helping and another glass of wine. It was so wonderful being here with him, she never wanted it to end, but she kept thinking I shouldn't be here. I shouldn't be enjoying myself like this. It's not fair on Adrian. This is how it was before. I let it go on because I loved him so much, and in the end I hurt him.

Nothing has changed. I've got to stop cheating him again . . .

When she offered to wash up, he said, 'No need. I leave that to Matty!'

'You have a housekeeper?' she asked, surprised.

He laughed and thumped the bench top. 'She lives under here. My automatic dishwasher! You've no need to be jealous.' He drew her into his arms as she straightened up from peering at the dishwasher. 'Chris . . .' His eyes were soft, beguiling her heart and tearing it to pieces both at once. 'Chris, marry me—*please*!'

Chris sagged in his arms. Suddenly it was all unbearable. She could stand the strain no longer and she broke down, clinging desperately to him, staining his shirt with tears while he held her close, murmuring, 'Chris, my darling, what is it? What is tearing you apart? I feel it all the time. Something between us you believe is insurmountable? What is it, Chris. Please let me help . . .'

She extricated herself from his embrace, ashamed of her loss of control. 'You can't help,' she said brokenly, 'no one can.'

His brow furrowed, his eyes darkened with anxiety. 'Chris, I might be able to, if only you would confide in me,' he pleaded.

She moistened her lips and steeled herself resolutely. 'You make the coffee and I'll stack the dishwasher,' she said. She fished in vain for a handkerchief and he dipped into a packet of paper tissues on the benchtop and handed her several. He was perplexed and saddened. What was making her like this? Seeing his concern wrenched every nerve in her body until she ached to her very core.

'It was a super meal, Adrian,' she said, trying to sound normal as she carefully placed the dirty dishes in the dishwasher. 'You're a very good cook.'

'I'm sure you're better. I hope you'll return the compliment. I gather you do wonders with a wok!'

The lightness of tone was false in both of them, and Chris did not look at him as she said, 'You must all come to my place for a meal soon. I was only saying to Janet the last time I was over there . . .' A surge of emotion made her break off. She closed the door of the dishwasher and set the dials and when it was operating, she went back to the family room. She held out her hands towards the pot-bellied stove although she wasn't cold. Only her hands were suddenly chill.

'This stove certainly makes the room lovely and warm.'

'Yes. It saves having to turn on the central heating if it's a little chilly at this time of year.'

Adrian brought the coffee in on a tray and when she heard the rattle as he placed it on the coffee table, she ceased prowling around looking at his pictures and ornaments. She felt calmer now. In the last few minutes she had finally found the courage she needed. He patted the cushion beside him inviting her to join him on the couch, but she ignored the gesture and instead stood rigidly holding her mug of coffee tightly in her hands to stop them from trembling.

'I have to tell you something,' she said. The conviction that she must had come suddenly. She had hoped to leave Mount William without Adrian ever finding out the truth, but she hadn't reckoned on his feelings for her reaching such a peak, or the intensity of her own for that matter. As she had waited for him to make the coffee an inner voice had said that now was the moment. For perhaps the first time there was an opportunity to talk about it. They were alone and not likely to be interrupted. She knew it was not going to be easy. She knew how Adrian would react and she didn't know whether she would be strong enough to resist him.

'Yes?' Apprehension put tension in his voice.

Chris took a deep breath. 'Lately I've begun to think that I should have told you eight years ago, but I didn't. I thought I was being noble, but really it was just cowardice. I'm sorry. If I'd told you then, you would have married and had a family by now. I never dreamed that you wouldn't. I feel very guilty about that.'

Fear grew and invaded every corner of his being. 'Chris, what are you trying to say?' He could think of nothing, no possibility that she might be leading up to that could give her so much pain to confess. He could think of nothing that he would not forgive her for.

Their eyes held for a moment and then Chris looked away.

'Chris,' Adrian said quietly. 'The only person I ever wanted to marry was you and nothing has changed. I don't care what dreadful secret you feel you must tell me, but it won't make the slightest difference. I shall still want to marry you.'

'Which is why I haven't told you before,' she said gravely, 'because I knew you might . . . and . . . I've been afraid I might not be strong-minded enough to refuse.'

His perplexity deepened. 'What on earth does that mean?'

Chris waited a moment, composing herself, and then the words poured out. 'If we married, Adrian, we would have no family. I would not be able to be mother of your children. I am not able to have children.'

The words hung in the air for a moment. Adrian slumped back against the cushions, as profoundly shocked as she had know he would be.

He said very quietly, looking intently at her. 'Are you certain?'

'Quite certain. It was salpingitis,' she said with grim brevity. 'I went to hospital with suspected appendicitis, but it wasn't . . .'

He closed his eyes briefly in further shock. When he was looking at her again he said in a strange hollow voice, 'You had surgery?'

'Yes.'

'When was this?'

'A few months before my finals. I never told anyone. I let everyone think it was appendicitis, even my family.'

'Chris . . .' His eyes were full of compassion. 'And

that's why you broke it off with me?'

She nodded. 'I should never have let things go so far. I—I didn't mean to get so involved, and then I tried to pretend it wouldn't matter.'

'It wouldn't have mattered!' he explained. 'Good God, Chris, what do you take me for?'

She looked at him sadly. It was just the reaction she'd expected, then as now. He would never admit his true yearning, even to himself. 'A very wonderful man,' she said simply, 'whom I had no right to deprive of his own flesh and blood children.'

'But every right apparently to deprive him of the woman he loves!'

'I didn't realise you felt so deeply, before,' she said. 'I thought you would soon get over it and find someone else. It wasn't easy, Adrian, but I believed it was the right thing to do, especially after . . . after someting you said . . .'

'What did I say?'

'You were telling me about your family and how close you all are. You said you couldn't wait to start a dynasty of your own and spend your old age surrounded by grandchildren and . . .'

'I was joking!'

'Were you? It's a natural wish. Instinct. I knew you were on the point of asking me to marry you and I panicked. I couldn't let you find out afterwards, and I was afraid if I told you first you would pretend it didn't matter, but that in the end you might have regretted it.'

'Chris!' He was outraged.

She resisted. 'Infertility often causes emotional problems in marriages. People blame each other. And you would have blamed me. I wasn't prepared to take that risk, Adrian. I'd seen you with children and knew how much you loved them—how much more you'd love your own. It wasn't all altruism on my part though. I couldn't bear running the risk of losing . . . of losing what I loved.'

Deep reproach shadowed his eyes. 'You didn't trust me.'

'It wasn't a question of trust. People fall in and out of

love all the time, especially when they're young. I was sure you'd find someone else.'

'Did you?' he asked drily.

Chris's mouth tightened. 'I never allowed myself to. I didn't want the same dilemma ever to arise again.' But looking at him now she knew with certainty that she never would have anyway.

He pulled her down beside him, holding her close, his heartbeat matching the rhythm of hers. He said, 'Chris . . . you crazy idiot! All these years wasted. If only I'd known, I'd never have let you go. Did it ever occur to you that we could have adopted children?'

'Of course it did. But I didn't think—still don't think—that would be fair. It's different when people marry and then find they can't conceive, but I already knew.'

He buried his face against her neck, his warm breath caressing her skin as he murmured softly, 'Chris, I don't care what noble intentions you still have, I am definitely not going to let you go again. You're going to marry me now whether you like it or not. I'm tired of being a bachelor, and there's never going to be any other woman for me. You're doing me out of even an adopted family if you refuse!'

Chris hardened her resolve. 'No, I am not going to marry you. Soon I will be going back to Mali and this time it will be different for you. No, don't argue with me. I know you mean what you're saying—now—but in time things will change. You'll get over it now you know the truth and you'll come to realise that my decision was the right one. You'll thank me for it one day.'

'Right!' he exploded. 'Bloody self-righteous, you mean! Thank you for it? Are you out of your mind? Chris, how can you do this to me? I love you, you love me. I don't give a cent piece about anything else. There's more to life than reproduction! Children are a bonus on love, not a downpayment!'

He pulled her roughly back into his arms, crushing her against him fiercely as he glared at her. 'I suppose you're getting a nice warm, self-sacrificial glow from all this altruism. Well, let me tell you . . .'

'Why are you making it so hard . . .?' she whispered, trying to free herself.

'I'm not! You are!'

In the struggle they sprawled across the couch with Adrian almost on top of her. His arms pinned her to the cushions and his mouth joined hers with an outpouring of passion such as she had never before experienced. Chris was incapable of resisting. She was more vulnerable than she had ever been and for a few moments there was nothing but the common fire that consumed them. Reason and logic had no place any more as this fierce exchange of love bound them more tightly together and brought them nearer to the ultimate fulfilment that both so urgently desired.

His hands beneath her sweater were warm against her skin, familiar and loving as he cradled her breasts in his palms, deliberately hardening her nipples between his fingers, while he smiled confidently at her, knowing only too well how easily his touch could set her on fire.

'Adrian, this is pointless . . .' she murmured.

'Is it?' he answered huskily. 'You never used to say that before, you used to rush into my arms as I did into yours . . .' His caresses made her senses cartwheel and when he pulled her closer and set about persuading her more puposefully, she felt herself slipping inexorably into the dangerous zone of believing it could work out all right . . .

He murmured insistently against her lips, 'You are going to marry me, Chris. I'm not letting you go again. I'm going to make you mine. *Mine—mine-mine*!' he said fiercely, kissing her hard between each word.

Chris felt her resistance dissolving as she had always been afraid it would. If he wanted her, she was his, for now, for tonight, for tomorrow, for every day and every night of the rest of their lives.

'Please let it last.' Her lips moved without a sound, her limbs twined with his and she pushed all her fears and doubts into the deepest recesses of her mind. He seemed to sense that she was no longer fighting him, either physically, mentally or emotionally. He moved a fraction away from her so he could look deeply into her face. 'Chris . . .?' he breathed softly, and began kissing her with a new tenderness that only gradually gave way to the passion he could not much longer contain.

Chris closed her eyes and slid her arms more tightly around him, and for a moment or two the loud shrilling in her ears did not even register. Adrian momentarily seemed unaware of it too, but telephones have a habit of persisting until they are answered, and doctors don't ignore ringing phones.

'Damn!' Adrian dragged his mouth from hers and the spell they had woven about themselves was cruelly shattered. He scowled. 'I'm not on call tonight. Neither are you.'

He dashed to answer it while Chris, feeling emotionally drained, rose and straightened her clothes. Her face burned and there was a numbness under her skin, while the ache of needing him still writhed inside her. She was a fool to have let him see how much she loved him, but now she wasn't sure she could regain her former resolve. The die had been cast in the past few minutes.

Adrian came back and his expression caused her to start in alarm. It was grey, gaunt, as though he'd had a terrible shock.

'Adrian, what is it?'

He seemed unable to speak, but after a moment he muttered hoarsely, 'It's Dad . . .'

'Oh, no!' Chris moved to him automatically, her hands reaching out.

'He collapsed an hour ago. They've taken him to hospital . . .' He seemed dazed.

'But he was progressing so well,' Chris said. It sounded fatuous to her ears. 'Oh, Adrian, we'd better go back, quickly.'

'Yes,' he said, 'yes, we'd better.'

They didn't talk much on the way back to Mount William. Adrian dropped Chris off at her house and drove on to the hospital. 'I'll let you know how things are as soon as I can,' were his parting words, and Chris caught the tremor in his voice and wished there was something useful she could do or say. She felt his anguish keenly. The Gilmores were a close family. She hoped Andrew's setback was not a serious one.

She watched the tail light of Adrian's car disappear at the end of her street and wished she hadn't added to his worries tonight. She went to bed with her thoughts full of anxiety for Adrian and his father, and a half fearful, half blissful anticipation of her own and Adrian's future.

# CHAPTER ELEVEN

CHRIS was forcing down breakfast, which she didn't feel like but she knew she must eat if she was to get through the day, when the phone rang. Feeling instinctively that it would be Adrian, she whipped the receiver off the hook. 'Adrian. .?' She spoke before he did.

'Chris. . .' From the tone of that one word she knew what the message was going to be, and she slumped into the chair beside the telephone, her teeth clamped on her bottom lip. 'He died this morning,' Adrian said, sounding incredulous. 'Mother and I were there, and Rachel.' His voice cracked and Chris said,

'I'm sorry. . .' How inadequate words were. How detached the telephone made one sound.

'They did everything possible,' Adian said, as though he was still trying to convince himself.

'I'm sure they did.' Chris searched for some words that would help, but found none. Her own emotions were too racked by the news. She hadn't known Andrew Gilmore long, but she'd a warm rapport with him, and with Janet too. They'd been kind to her, treating her almost like their own daughter.

'How's Janet?' she asked. 'Can I do anything?' It seemed that there were only platitudes to offer.

'Mother's not quite taken it in yet,' he answered. 'It was so sudden. She's being very stoical at the moment. You know, saying she's glad he didn't suffer, that sort of thing. The reaction will set in later, but Rachel's with her and the others will be coming as soon as they can. I guess I'll be a bit tied up for a couple of days. Will you tell them at the Centre for me, please, Chris? You can call me any time, of course, in an emergency.'

Chris said at once, 'Do whatever you have to do, Adrian and don't worry about the Centre. We'll cope.

164

People will understand.'

'I'll see you later, then,' he said, and Chris heard the upswell of emotion in his voice. She wanted to spare him the embarrassment of breaking down, so she said quickly,

'Sure. I'll let you know if anything crops up that requires your attention specially.' She added, 'Give my love to your mother, and please let me know if there's anything I can do.'

'You'll be doing it, helping to keep the wheels turning at the Centre,' Adrian said gratefully. 'Thanks a million, though, Chris. I appreciate it, and so will she.' There was a slight pause, then more in control, he said, 'Will you come to the funeral? Mother'd appreciate that too.'

'Of course I will,' Chris anwered softly.

'I'll let you know the details later. 'Bye now, and Chris. . . take care.' A click and he was gone.

She knew she shouldn't, but she couldn't help feeling disappointed he had not even briefly referred to last night. If he'd only called her 'darling'. She felt afraid suddenly as though she must have mistaken a dream for reality after all.

During the next few days Chris saw very little of Adrian and her fears grew. When they did cross paths it was only very briefly. He dashed into the medical centre once or twice, and on one of these occasions she only caught a glimpse of him between consultations when she happened to go out to the office for some reason just as he was leaving. He did not call at her home.

She was him at the funeral, of course, and he made a special point of introducing her to his brothers and sisters whom she had not met before, but he lingered himself only to exchange a few words. Chris knew he was preoccupied and anxious about Janet, but she felt suddenly that he was avoiding her eyes and that he did not want to touch on personal subjects.

She thought she knew why. He'd had time, in spite of his grief, to think things over. In the cold clear light of reality he had begun to see things differently. She was sure that he regretted his rashness that night at Ravensbush. He had faced up to what marrying her would mean and had realised that despite his emotional involvement with her, the kind of future they would have together was not what he wanted.

I ought to be glad, she thought, that he's realised it now before it's too late. But for her it was already too late. She had been ready to take the risk. During the past months she had come to love him more deeply than she had when she'd first known him. It was not a case of old wounds having been re-opened, it was a case of new and deeper wounds having been inflicted.

Chris wondered several times if she ought to go and see Janet, but she did not want to add to Adrian's anguish, and in any case, several members of the family were either staying or coming and going, and she didn't want to intrude. She sent as comforting a letter as she could write.

Long hours at the Centre left Chris exhausted in the evenings, and she was grateful for this as it gave her less time to brood and regret that she had ever been foolish enough to take on this job in Mount William.

When Adrian came back full-time, Chris still saw very little of him and she was sure that he avoided being alone with her, or even having a lengthy conversation. If they met in the lounge when no one else was present he always seemed to have an excuse for disappearing quickly. Chris found herself avoiding him too.

So the first real news Chris had of Janet Gilmore, apart from a couple of brief reassurances from Adrian that she was bearing up, during the first couple of weeks after the funeral, came not from him but, surprisingly, from Rita Vanderhoek.

Late one evening, Chris found herself dashing out on an emergency call to Mrs Forster, the elderly asthma patient she had visited before with Rita. As they both had expected, her condition had deteriorated and now a crisis had occurred. It was a wonder she had managed to pick up the phone and summon help.

Mrs Forster's spasm had subsided when Chris arrived at the house, just ahead of the ambulance and Rita, whom she'd phoned before leaving her own house, but the old lady was in a very distressed state and in immediate need of the oxygen which the ambulance provided. Her collapse was partly due to the bronchopneumonia which Chris and Rita had feared would eventually develop.

There was no resistance about going to hospital now. But as the ambulance men laid her on the stretcher she looked imploringly at Chris and Rita and whispered, 'Fred and Smokey. . .'

Chris clasped the gnarled old hand and reassured her, 'Don't worry, Mrs Forster. We'll take care of them.'

Mrs Forster relaxed. The bluish, almost transparent skin made her look very fragile. Chris felt confident, though, that with careful nursing she would soon be back on her feet again.

Later, having a cup of coffee with Rita at the hospital, after having seem Mrs Forster settled in intensive care, Chris mentioned the old lady's pets.

'It's important for her peace of mind to know they're being looked after,' Chris said.

Rita offered, 'I can pop in and feed them for a few days until we find someone who'll look after them.'

'When this came up before Adrian said he'd ask his mother,' Chris remembered, 'but it wasn't necessary because Mrs Forster refused to budge then. Perhaps we should ask Janet now.'

'Shall I mention it to him or will you?' Rita asked.

Chris ran weary fingers through her hair. All at once she didn't want to talk to Adrian about anything. 'You'll probably see him first,' she said, without any particular reason to think so.

Then Rita dropped her bombshell. 'I suppose he told you he's moving into a unit in my block soon?'

Chris's head came up and she looked at Rita in amazement. 'He is? But why would he do that?'

Rita seemed surprised she didn't already know. 'His mother's selling the house and moving to Ballarat. She's going to stay with her daughter until she can find a suitable unit. Adrian said she's already seen one she likes and hopes to buy it and be in by Christmas.'

Chris was completely taken aback. There hadn't even been a whisper of all this at the Centre so far as she knew and Adrian had certainly said nothing to her. Rita's cheeks were slightly flushed and Chris wondered if there was any significance in Adrian's moving into the same block of flats.

She said, 'Well, if you've got Adrian next door, you'll be able to keep an eye on him!'

Rita sighed and looked soulful. 'I wish he'd let me!' she said. Then she asked casually, 'Are you still going back to Africa?'

'I hope so,' answered Chris. 'I'll be here until Christmas and I expect to fly out to Mali early in the New Year.' She wondered if she imagined the fleeting look of relief that crossed the district nurse's face.

They left the hospital together and went their separate way home. Chris spent a night of sleep disturbed by dreams of Adrian and the tall blonde district nurse, and in the morning as she wearily ate breakfast, she was shocked at the dark waves of jealousy that assailed her. But at least Rita was preferable to Deborah Leigh, she tried to console herself.

She hadn't seen Deborah for some time, but she cropped up in conversation when Janet Gilmore invited her round one evening just before she left Mount William to live in Ballarat. Chris was relieved to find that Adrian was not at home.

'He's gone to Deborah Leigh's engagement party,' Janet said, and amused by Chris's surprise, explained, 'She's marrying a wealthy Western Districts grazier. She's having a big do on the property. Marquees, jazz band and all that.' She made a wry face. Janet had never approved of Deborah as a wife for Adrian, so she was undoubtedly glad she was now out of circulation.

'I hope Adrian wasn't too upset,' Chris said, fishing.

'Oh, no, I don't think so. There's someone else he's much more interested in.'

It must be Rita, thought Chris, only Janet won't say so directly because she isn't sure how I feel about him.

They talked about Janet's plans for the future and Chris's return to Mali. Both shed a few tears over Andrew, but Janet was, Chris thought, remarkably self-controlled and determined that her life would still have some meaning even without her beloved husband.

There was a sharp pang for Chris when Janet mentioned Rita directly, but only in connection with Mrs Forster.

'Addie Forster thinks the sun shines out of that girl,' Janet said. 'She looked after her pets when she was in hospital and even put seed out for the birds, and found her a home help so she can stay on in her own home for the time being anyway.'

'Rita's a very kind person,' Chris said. She already knew that Rita had decided not to bother Adrian or Janet with Mrs Forster's problems but had solved them herself.

Janet twinkled. 'Old Addie had nothing but praise for you too, my dear.'

'I didn't do much for her.'

'Yes, you did. You went to her promptly when she had that bad attack, and she appreciates your popping in to see how she is now then without being asked.'

Chris flushed. 'I've only been there three or four times. She always mentions how thoughtful Rita is.' She was dying to ask now if Rita was the person Adrian was interested in, but she couldn't bring herself to say the words. Because she knew in her heart what the answer would be.

As Chris was leaving, Janet mentioned that a doctor friend of Adrian's was coming up the next day to look around with a view to joining the practice.

Adrian brought him into the lounge at lunchtime to meet the other members of the practice and Chris was, along with Paul and Graham, introduced.

Mark Farnham was, it appeared, considering joining on a permanent basis, not just as a locum, Chris chatted to him for a few minutes, but all the time she was conscious of Adrian's gaze drifting across her face. When their eyes met, however, there was no clue in the dark brown depths of his as to what he was thinking.

A few days later she heard that Dr Farnham and his young family would be coming to Mount William after Christmas. This was news served as a sharp remindedr to Chris that her days were now numbered and that very soon she would leaving Mount William and her months in the Central Highlands town would fade into memory as she took up her other life again.

Painful though it had been, perhaps, she sometimes thought, she had been meant to come to Mount William. It hadn't been an easy road, but she had at last told Adrian the truth, and she had freed him from the chains that subconsciously bound him to her.

Sometimes she wondered what might have happened if his father had not died. Would things have turned out differently if they had not been interrupted that night? Would the future have been just as she had feared? It almost seemed that fate had intervened. She wished it hadn't been in such a tragic way, though.

His father's death had given Adrian breathing space. It had forcibly distanced him from Chris for long enough to enable him to think dispassionately about the whole situation. Instead of making a hasty emotional commitment to her, he'd been forced to stand back and see it all in perspective.

The flaring of their attraction for each other had been understandable, but irrational. She was sure that he must realise that now, and that his needs were wider and deeper than the mere physical attraction, even the strong emotional caring, he felt for her. By coming to Mount William she had helped him to lay the ghost that had inhibited his relationships with other women. Rita would undoubtedly be the beneficiary of that, Chris thought wistfully. And she would bear him lots of lovely children.

\* \* \*

A few days before Chris left the town, Rose and Duncan MacLeod threw a farewell party for her. It was a lively affair in the local Mechanics Institute Hall, but Chris had to make a superhuman effort to appear cheerful. She hadn't felt so depressed since her illness. Nevertheless she dressed up for the occasion, buying a new dark red dress that she hoped would boost her morale, and she threw herself wholeheartedly into dancing with anyone and everyone who asked her. She even flirted a little with Paul — it didn't matter now. She'd been windsurfing with him lately a few times at Lake Fyans, but they were simply good friends.

He said half seriously, 'If I was thinking of getting married, I'd chance asking you, Chris. You do things to me most women never do!'

'Like sober you up?' she teased.

'I was never so embarrassed,' he said. 'I could hardly look at you for weeks.' He pulled her close and she momentarily rested her head against his shoulder, a wave of regret at leaving suddenly washing over her. Then she saw Adrian dancing past and he seemed to be glowering at her.

He had not danced with her yet and she was beginning to wonder if he would. She was nervous of it, unsure whether her carefully cultivated composure would stand the strain of being pysically close to him. She watched him dancing with Rita, and it was obvious that the district nurse had a certain glow about her.

'It won't be the same without you, Chris,' said Rose sadly. 'We'll all miss you.'

Chris was touched. There were other compliments too until she felt embarrassed, and when she was presented with a solid silver St Christopher medal to protect her on her travels, she almost wept. It was suddenly borne on her how deeply rooted in the town she had become, how much she felt she belonged. There was unexpected anguish in having to leave.

Carole said in a half serious tone. 'I can't believe you're going, Chris, I was sure you'd end up staying for keeps.'

'I only came as a locum,' Chris reminded her.

Carole rolled her eyes. 'I know, but I had a bet with Rose that you and Adrian would marry.'

'Well, you lost that bet!' said Chris, trying to sound lighthearted.

'Sure did. Although maybe he'll miss you so much, he'll take the next plane to Mali. Now that would be romantic!'

'I think he's a little too preoccupied pursuing someone else, Carole.'

Carole glanced across at Adrian and Rita who were chatting animatedly. 'You mean Rita? Well, I reckon she fancies him, but who doesn't? Look at Deborah Leigh. She gave up and got engaged to someone else in the end. Maybe he's just the bachelor type after all.'

A hand fell on Chris's shoulder. 'You haven't danced with me yet, Chris.'

She wanted to say, 'Only because you haven't asked me,' but she smiled at him instead.

Carole winked broadly at Chris and said, 'Excuse me, while I chat up the hospital's new anaesthetist. He's just what I need to brighten up my dull life!'

Adrian guided Chris on to the floor. He didn't speak for a few moments, and she just submerged herself in the wonderful feeling being in his arms again gave her. It might only be a duty dance, but for Chris it was happiness. She refused to acknowledge the pain that went with it. She wondered if now, at the last minute, he might suddenly feel compelled to broach the subject of their relationship and apologise. She hoped he wouldn't, because she knew she wouldn't be able to speak about it without breaking down.

'When are you off back to Mali?' he asked eventually, and she knew he was not going to touch on their personal involvement.

She gave an inward sigh of relief. 'I don't know yet,' she replied. 'I've written to Wayne at the Foundation in Sydney saying I'm available from January, but I haven't had a reply yet. My medical passed me A1,' she added with a smile. She had dashed down to Melbourne for it only a couple of weeks ago.

'See you keep it that way,' Adrian cautioned, with a flash of concern lighting his eyes. 'You're looking forward to going back?'

'Oh, yes. It's been a long time. Some of the people I worked with won't still be there, unfortunately, as their contracts will have expired, but I expect there'll be a few familiar faces.'

'Most people stay only a couple of years, I gather, but you chose to stay longer?'

'I'm not the only one. The Director's been there for years and years. And there are others. We have a steady backbone, fortunately.'

He held her close but not too close and lightly ran his fingers down her spine. 'You have a strong backbone, Chris,' he said softly, and she hoped he wasn't aware of the tremor his fingers were causing.

'How is your mother?' she asked. She had not seen Janet Gilmore since she had moved to Ballarat. 'Is she settling in all right?'

'Yes, she seems to be. It's a bit of a madhouse at Rachel's place, so she'll be glad to move into her unit and have some privacy again.'

'She must miss your father terribly,' Chris said sadly.

'They were married for nearly forty years,' Adrian told her. 'That's quite a long time.'

'It will take time for her to adjust.'

Oh, heavens, she thought, despite the seriousness of it, we're still only making polite conversation, behaving like acquaintances. We've said all this before. We can't be natural with each other any more.

This may be almost the last time I shall see him, Chris thought suddenly, and certainly the last time he'll hold me in his arms. Tears filled her eyes and she blinked vigorously to dispel them, hoping Adrian would not notice.

'You're spending Christmas with your family?' he was

saying.

'Yes.' She tried valiantly to keep the emotion out of her voice. 'It will be the first time for several years, so it'll be quite a celebration.'

# CHAPTER TWELVE

CHRIS was at home in Melbourne a few days before Christmas. Despite a heatwave that threatened to turn it into one of the hottest ever, her mother was still determined to have a traditional celebration. She was not prepared to be so radical as to have a vegetarian Christmas dinner for everyone, but she compromised by buying only free-range poultry and eggs, and forgoing ham.

Chris was pleased that the plight of intensively farmed animals had made even that much impression. She had never expected to change people overnight, all she could do was hope for a dawning of compassion. She smiled to herself when she saw her mother poring over a recipe for a soya bean loaf which she stubbornly refused to let Chris make herself for her Christmas dinner.

'I like experimenting,' she insisted, with a smile, and added, 'I made one a while ago and your father loved it!'

Two days before Christmas, Chris went into the city to do some last-minute shopping for her mother and herself. It was hot, but despite the heat the crowds milled around as thick as ever.

It would be even worse tomorrow, she thought, glad she had decided to come today. Feeling exhausted after a couple of hours, she stopped for a rest in the Bourke Street mall. She sank on to a seat in the shade of a plane tree, her carrier bags clustered around her aching feet. She consulted her list and struck off the purchases already made. Only a few small items remained.

'Thank goodness!' Chris sighed, and leaned back, relaxing for a few moments. She decided that she would get a taxi home. Struggling on to a tram with all her shopping would be a nightmare.

As her eyes drifted slowly around the scene in the mall and she idly watched a busker performing, in an unguarded moment she let her thoughts wander away from Christmas shopping. What was Adrian doing now? Would he be spending Christmas in Ballarat? Or would he be with Rita . . .?

As she tried to close off the thoughts that made her heart ache so painfully and her gaze shifted to the other side of the mall, she stiffened. As though in answer to her thoughts, two familiar figures strolled along the footpath. Adrian and Rita.

Rita, in a sleeveless linen dress, with her blonde hair cut short instead of in her usual severe chignon, and wearing more make-up than usual, looked slimmer and prettier than Chris remembered, although it was only a week since she'd seen her. Rita's blonde hair and lightly tanned skin were shown to advantage by the smart lime green dress she was wearing and her legs looked so much more shapely in high-heeled white sandals than in the sensible shoes she normally wore. There was a vivaciousness about her, Chris thought, that could only mean one thing—she was in love.

She's really very pretty, Chris thought, and was ashamed of the swift surge of jealousy that assailed her.

Rita was chatting avidly to Adrian. Chris let her eyes rest on his face, and her heart lurched with longing. He looked happier, she thought, than she'd seen him look for weeks. And so handsome in light tan trousers, a casual cream linen jacket. He was smiling at Rita. They looked like a very happy couple.

Neither looked in her direction. Rita paused, then caught Adrian's arm and said something, pointing towards a shop they were passing. They turned and walked into it. It was a jeweller's, with one window sparkling with rings. Was Adrian's Christmas gift to Rita to be an engagement ring? Tears welled up in Chris's eyes.

'I'm glad,' she whispered, trying hard to mean it. 'I'm glad . . .'

'Letter for you, dear,' her mother said when she arrived home by taxi some time later.

When she saw the envelope's Sydney postmark, Chris slit it open eagerly. It was, as she hoped, from the Foundation. She read it with a sigh of relief.

'I'm going back!' she said jubilantly. 'I've got another two-year contract with an option to renew. Isn't that marvellous?'

'Oh, Chris . . . do you really have to go?' Her mother was not so enthusiastic.

'I must,' Chris affirmed. She didn't say that now there was another reason why she wanted to go. She needed to be very far away from Adrian. 'Don't worry,' she consoled, giving her mother an affectionate hug, 'I'll be back again before you've had time to miss me. It's a condition of my contract that I take regular home leave.' She passed the letter to her mother to read.

'Of course I want you to do what you want to do, Chris,' said Ellen Hart, 'but I confess I was wishing you and that nice doctor Adrian Gilmore would get together again . . .'

'You're a romantic, Mum!' admonished Chris with a laugh she had to force. 'Didn't I tell you? Adrian's going to marry a nice District Nurse from Mount William. I'm betting they get engaged for Christmas.'

Her mother looked not only disappointed, but anxious too. 'Would you have married him if he'd asked you, Chris?' she dared to ask.

Chris tried to keep her tone light and give nothing away. 'No.'

Ellen, however, caught the slight trembling at the corners of her mouth and wondered. 'When will you be leaving?' she asked.

'End of January,' said Chris, pointing to the paragraph in the letter.

'Yes—yes, I wasn't taking it in,' said Ellen. 'Well, at least you'll be here until New Year and for a bit longer.'

Christmas came and went, and Chris endured it all with

part of her joining in the festivities, part of her detached.
She did all the things expected of her automatically. She
took her young nieces and nephews to Carols by
Candlelight and the beach, to cinemas and shopping.
They all went on family picnics and other outings. Chris
enjoyed being involved in the family again, yet all the
time she felt apart from them all.

Once she was back in Mali, she kept thinking, the pain
would fade. Hard work and other people's infinitely
worse agonies would help her to forget Adrian and stop
wallowing in self-pity. And this time she would not be
plagued with might-have-beens. It would be really and
truly over at last.

Between Christmas and New Year, Janet Gilmore
phoned.

'Chris I'm so glad to have caught you. Did you have a
happy Christmas?'

'Lovely, thanks. And you?'

'Hectic! All the family were here—Rachel's house and
my unit were bursting at the seams, but we managed. We
missed Andrew dreadfully, of course, but we didn't have
time to brood and we knew he wouldn't have wanted us
to be sad.'

They talked about Christmas and Janet's new home
for a few minutes and then Janet said, 'I was hoping to
get down to Melbourne for a couple of days soon and I'd
like to see you before you leave, but I'm looking after
their house while Rachel and Dan and the children are
away for most of January. The garden needs watering
every day this weather. I know you haven't much time
left with your family, but could you possibly spare a day
to come up here?'

Chris couldn't say no. And she wanted very much to
say goodbye to Janet. 'I'm sure I can,' she said. 'When
would suit you? I leave on the thirtieth.'

'What about the second or third, when we've all got
over New Year?' suggested Janet.

'That would be fine,' Chris agreed, and then asked
casually, 'How is everybody?' Janet had not mentioned

Adrian or Rita when she had been talking about Christmas, nothing about an engagement. Perhaps she was afraid Chris might be hurt by the news.

'Fine, just fine,' said Janet. There was a slight pause, then she went on hurriedly, 'I'm sorry, Chris, I'll have to go—there's someone at the front door. Come up as early as you can and stay overnight. It'll be good to have a nice long chat.'

Afterwards Chris reflected that Janet had surely ended the conversation abruptly because she did not want to be asked too many penetrating questions.

It was not until after dinner on the night Chris spent in Ballarat that she had the courage to mention Adrian and Rita again. Janet had not said a word about them, and it was gnawing at Chris unbearably. She had to know.

'I saw Adrian and Rita in Melbourne when I was Christmas shopping,' she plunged in with at last. 'They were going into a jeweller's shop.'

Janet gave her a swift, surprised look. 'Adrian didn't say he'd seen you.'

'He didn't. I-I was in a hurry. I couldn't stop to say hello to them.'

Janet said, 'Adrian did mention that he'd given Rita a lift to Melbourne just before Christmas. She's a nice girl. She helped him choose my clock.' She pointed to a clock on the wall. 'Adrian's Christmas gift, an electric clock. I never have to wind it! I expect he bought it in the jeweller's you saw them going into.'

Chris gulped. Perhaps they hadn't become engaged after all. Janet poured more coffee into Chris's cup. 'It's a pity Rita'a leaving Mount William.'

'Leaving?' Chris was astonished.

'Yes, she's moving to Horsham soon. Her fiancé lives there.'

If Janet was aware of the shocks she was giving Chris she gave no sign. Chris said, 'You mean, Rita's engaged? That was a bit sudden, wasn't it?'

'Not really. Apparently she'd been going around with

some fellow for quite a while and they split up for some reason. Over Christmas it seems they got together again and he popped the question. So Adrian said the other day.'

'Is-is he very upset?' Chris had to ask.

Janet's face was unrevealing. 'That she's leaving? Yes, I dare say he is. She's very good at her job. One of the nurses from the hospital is going to take over, I believe.'

'But I was under the impression—well, I thought Adrian and Rita . . . had lately . . .' Chris floundered. 'Well, I thought they were more than just friends.'

'Did you?' Janet said, sounding surprised. 'I never thought that. I don't think Adrian was ever interested in her even if she was in him. His attentions have been occupied elsewhere.'

'Oh?' But Deborah was out of the picture, so who?

'As a matter of fact, he hopes to be getting married soon,' Janet confided, her shrewed eyes weighing up Chris thoughtfully.

Chris was having difficulty sounding casual. 'Anyone I know?'

'You could probably guess,' Janet said tantalisingly. 'He's been in love with her for years.'

Which surely meant it had to be Deborah, Chris thought. She must have broken off her engagement. Maybe she'd only got engaged to someone else to make Adrian jealous.

'Deborah Leigh?' she asked tentatively.'

'Deborah? Heavens, no!' exclaimed Janet. 'She's still engaged to her grazier, thank goodness.' She added firmly, 'I think he'd rather I didn't say any more until it's official.'

And so Chris was left speculating. One of the nurses at the hospital? There were other eligible females in Mount William, but she didn't know all his friends. And he had friends in Melbourne too.

'Now let's talk about your plans,' Janet said, clearly eager to drop the subject of her son.

They did not mention Adrian again and when Chris

went to bed she was still puzzling over Janet's cryptic remarks. Why couldn't she tell her? It wasn't as though she could blurt it out to anyone Adrian knew.

Chris was awake early. The night had been long and storm tossed with tantalising dreams, and more than once Chris's pillow had been dampened by tears. She woke determined to put it all behind her. She must close the door very firmly on Adrian Gilmore after today. Whom he married was of no interest to her.

She pulled on a pair of white jeans and a red and white striped shirt and red sandals. She heard sounds in the kitchen as she crossed the hall and pushed open the door. "Morning, Janet,' she said breezily to the figure bending over the sink, then stopped dead.

'Sorry, she's just taken the dogs for a walk.' It was Adrian who turned round, coffee-pot in hand. 'Like some coffee?'

Chris nearly fainted. 'Adrian! What are you doing here?'

'I drove down last night and slept at Rachel's. I came to see you, Chris.'

His dark eyes regarded her intently for a moment, then he smiled, a slow, heart-melting smile and pointed to a sheet of paper beside an envelope on the table. 'Read that and you'll see why.'

Chris, mystified, picked up the single sheet of paper. Her eyes flicked incredulously across the letterhead. Australian Medical Aid Foundation. With racing heart she read the contents. The brisk, no-nonsense style of the Director, Wayne Rogers, was unmistakable. Chris strung bits of it together in her mind, the bits that hit her with the impact of a steamroller.

' . . . pleased to confirm your appointment as a Senior Medical Officer at our Mali headquarters.' ' . . . understand you wish to travel with Dr Hart on January 30. No reason why not providing that gives you time to arrange passport, marriage licence etc.' 'Congratulations to you both. I have unequivocal confidence in you as a team, both medically and matrimonially. All the best,

Wayne.'

Chris swallowed and looked at Adrian. She caught the tail-end of his anxiety before it turned to a smile again and he said, 'Sit down, Chris, we've got quite a bit to say before Mother gets back. Coffee? Or would you like orange juice first?'

'Orange juice, please,' said Chris faintly. She slid weakly into a chair, not comprehending. Was this some sort of dream she was still in? She rested her elbows on the table and watched in stunned silence as Adrian poured a glass of orange juice and handed it to her. She took it in trembling fingers and gulped a large mouthful.

'You seem to have been very busy . . .' she faltered.

He was still uncertain. Had he gone too far before talking to her again? Had he taken too much for granted by confronting her with a fait accompli? His stomach was twisted into a tight knot. But he wasn't going to give in easily. He wanted Chris for his wife. He had wanted her ever since he'd met her more than eight years ago. He wasn't going to let anything prevent them from being together for the rest of their lives. He thought it now as he'd thought it every day, every night, for the past few weeks while his plan was fermenting and letters and phone calls were speeding back and forth. In a moment he would tell her all about that. When the facts had had a chance to sink in.

'There wasn't much to do at the Centre,' he said, with a quirky grin. 'People were mercifully healthy over Christmas, and now most of them are off on holidays. I had to occupy my time somehow!'

A glimmer of a smile played around Chris's lips. She was filled with a kind of stupefying wonder that he would go to such lengths.

'Adrian, you can't do this,' she said at last. 'You can't possibly . . .'

'It's done,' he said calmly, dropping slices of bread into the toaster. 'You wouldn't have to tell Wayne it was all a big mistake, would you? I'd look such a fool!'

Chris bit her lip. 'It was unethical . . .'

'It was the only way to make you see sense!' The dark brown eyes burned into hers and a warm sensation spread tentacles all through her.

She spread her palms upwards on the table, staring at them as though reading the lines on them would convince her that this was pre-ordained. She wasn't quite sure how she felt at the moment. She was overwhelmed, her feelings for him had never been so powerful, and yet her fears were not entirely diminished. Adrian had made this grand gesture to try and convince her, but was it just that, a grand gesture, a big heart-warming show of fidelity despite everythng? That night at Ravensbush, she had been willing to take chances but she'd been carried away by emotion then.

'Adrian, you can't just chuck up everything and go out there because of me. What about the practice—your vineyard—Janet?'

'Stop! You'll make me feel guilty as well as self-righteous in a minute! And I assure you I'm neither! I'm just a man who knows what he wants. And I want you, Chris. I want to share your life, to have you at my side for all time. My life has been empty without you. I venture to hope that yours has been somewhat lack-lustre without me! I thought about it long and hard after Dad died and my conclusion was always the same. The most important thing in my life was you. It wasn't just an emotional decision. It was made in the harsh light of reality, with the knowledge that you expected nothing of me. I examined myself from your point of view. But the answer was always the same.'

He sat down and took her helplessly flexing fingers firmly between his large hands. He raised them to his lips. 'I love you, Chris. You must believe that.' Tears welled up in her eyes and she chewed her bottom lip trying to banish them. The toast popped up, startling them.

'The-the toast . . .' Chris stammered foolishly.

'Hang the bloody toast!' exclaimed Adrian, and then

chuckled. 'You always were practical!'

He rose and removed the slices and flung them into a plate, pushing it towards her. 'Marmalade?'

It couldn't be happening, Chris thought. Not like this, not over something as prosaic as breakfast. Suddenly she was smiling through her tears. 'Oh, Adrian!' she cried, and leaping up, flung herself into his arms. 'Oh, my love . . .'

His arms folded around her and he held her shaking body close and closed his eyes in a silent prayer of thanks to any deity that might be listening. He had the wonderful, ecstatic feeling that he had won.

Chris felt his heart beating strongly against hers and the warmth of him seeping through to her. His chin nuzzled the top of her head, and after a moment, he tipped her head up and kissed her, a long kiss of such exquisite tenderness that she felt she might melt away at his feet. There was no raging passion in the kiss, only the gentleness of relief and discovery and the joy of declaring their love without restraint.

'Chris . . .' Adrian threaded his fingers through her hair. 'Chris, my darling girl . . . I can hardly believe it . . . you're in my arms again. And this time I'm never going to let you go.'

'I think I must be dreaming,' Chris murmured, and turned to look at the letter again. 'Adrian, you can't do this . . .'

He silenced her with a kiss. 'Why not? I've always wanted to work overseas, but I never got around to doing anything positive about it. When I was away recently, however, it was in my mind again, but not crystallised. I heard a lot about conditions in some of the African countries first-hand at one of my conferences. But it seems I had to wait for the right moment to act, for the opportunity to arise. Your coming back into my life provided it.'

'But what are you going to do about the practice, about everything else?' Chris asked again, bewildered by the enormity of what he was proposing.

'Eat your breakfast and I'll tell you.'

Chris slid reluctantly out of his arms and sat down again. Adrian poured coffee and slid more bread into the toaster, although it was unlikely they would eat it. Chris was hardly able to take her eyes from his face, as though if she did, he might vanish.

'It's simple,' said Adrian. 'When Dad died, it was a turning point for Mother and me. It was the moment when, if things were to change, it had to be then. Everything seemed to point me in the direction I subconsciously wanted to go.

'Mother wanted to move to Ballarat, so I was relieved of any responsibility for her. Then I had a letter from Mark Farnham, an old acquaintance, who was anxious to take up practice in a country town. He wrote and asked if I knew of anywhere. Naturally I offered him Mount William. The practice will need another full-time doctor too, but they can manage with locums meanwhile.'

'And you knew Wayne . . .' Chris remembered.

'Yes. I got in touch with him and told him what I wanted to do. He was very helpful.' He grinned at her. 'I'm quite good at string-pulling! Everything, you see, seemed to slot into place as though it were preordained.'

'And you were already making these plans before I left Mount William, yet you never breathed a word to me,' Chris murmured. 'I thought you were avoiding me because . . .' She broke off, not wanting to say she'd believed he had changed his mind, that she'd thought he'd turned his attention to Rita.

'I was! How could I tell you what I was doing? I wasn't at all sure I'd convinced you that night at Ravensbush that you were my first priority and nothing else mattered. I had to try and prove it to you somehow.' He reached for her hand. 'Chris, I'm a doctor and there are millions of children who need me more than I need children of my own. What I do need that no one else can give me is your love . . .'

'I seem to have gravely underestimated you—and

misjudged you,' Chris murmured.

Adrian leaned across the table and kissed her mouth. 'You certainly underestimated me, my darling. I'm a devil for manipulating people when I want to!'

'You certainly excelled yourself this time!'

He grimaced. 'I had one horrible moment at your farewell party when you were dancing with Paul. It looked as though it might be on again. You'd been going out together again, I knew.'

'Paul had been teaching me to wind-surf, that's all,' Chris confessed. 'I needed something to occupy my mind, and time. It was never "on" with him anyway!' she added indignantly.

'So he told me,' Adrian said apologetically, and seeing her astounded expression. 'If it had been, I was sure it could only be temporary, but even that would have cast doubts on what I believed about how you felt about me. I didn't want to make a complete fool of myself. I had to ask him.' There was a lengthy pause, then he said seriously, 'Chris, you haven't said you've forgiven me yet, or that you'll marry me.'

'Do I need to,' she answered gently. 'Can't you tell?'

'I want to hear you say it. I want to hear the words from your lips, to savour them . . .' he murmured teasingly.

'You fool! All right, I forgive you and I can't wait to marry you, but I think I'll press for a rider in the marriage service which says that although I promise to obey most of the time, I won't tolerate unilateral decisions!'

He kissed her hard. 'Sealed! I promise that never again will I trick you into doing what I'm sure you want to do anyway!'

'Your toast is going soggy,' Chris said, feeling a lightness of spirit such as she had not known for years. She felt like a bird that has been caged and finally learns how to fly again. She felt as though she was soaring up into the sky on a joyous flight of freedom.

'And you are dripping marmalade down your chin.'

'I have developed disgusting habits living alone,' she warned, with a twinkle in her grey eyes now. 'You have no idea what you're letting yourself in for.'

He chuckled. 'Do you? I have recently become very domineering and possessive, and if another man so much as flirts with you . . . I could have hospitalised Paul for even looking at you!'

'You still haven't told me what you plan to do about the vineyard. You'll miss it terribly. And your beautiful house.'

'It will be there for us to come home to,' he said gently. 'Wayne told me he's insisting you have regular home leave and naturally I'll come with you. Robert and Faye will look after Ravensbush for us and my family will continue to holiday there. One day, perhaps we will come back permanently. Meanwhile, who knows, we may even start our adopted family in Africa! But let's not try to plan the future too rigidly, Chris. Fate has a habit of arranging our lives, it seems, to suit her capricious self. Let's take each day as it comes and savour it, and let the future be a voyage of discovery with not too detailed maps. We don't want a package tour, do we?'

'Heaven forbid!' she said fervently, and with a suspicious glint in her eyes, 'Adrian, your mother knows all about this, doesn't she?'

'Of course! And she said that an hour and a half was as long as she was prepared to spend walking the dogs. She said if I couldn't persuade you in that time, I didn't deserve you!'

'She'll miss you,' Chris warned.

'Sometimes, no doubt, but she has her own future to consider now, a future without Dad. She has family around her. And this is what she wanted. She's enjoyed being involved in the final conspiracy!'

Adrian glanced at his watch. 'She's been gone about an hour and twenty minutes, so if I'm going to kiss my future bride properly, in private . . .'

He stood up and pulled her into his arms. 'Do you

think we can get married by the thirtieth? It won't be too much of a rush?'

Chris, with a straight face, said, 'Perhaps it is—maybe we should just see how things work out first—how you feel in a few months . . .'

'Chris!' Adrian crushed her in a rib-cracking bear-hug, and she gloried in the hardness of his body, the possessiveness of his encircling arms. 'Don't you dare suggest such a thing! Otherwise I shall drag you off to church in chains with a pistol at your head.'

'Well, that would be novel!' she laughed, and laid her head against his chest. 'Adrian, I'm just so . . . so scared this is all going to turn out not to be true after all.'

His lips gentled hers with a kiss that both aroused and reassured her. 'Trust me, Chris. I promise with all my heart that I'll never let you down.'

'I think we could easily get married before the thirtieth,' she whispered. 'We don't want a lot of fuss, do we? We could have the ceremony in the garden at my parents' home—what do you think . . .?'

Adrian's mouth covered hers and his lips opened on hers as the echo of her last word left them, but the kiss was only a fleeting one. The sound of a key in the door of the unit startled them apart and they stood in a kind of bemused daze as the dogs galloped in, followed by a breathless, but rather tentative Janet.

She swept an anxious look across their faces, then hers relaxed and she smiled with relief.

'Oh, good, I can see I *have* interrupted something! Congratulations!'

Chris and Adrian looked at each other and burst out laughing.